HEAR YE! HEAR YE!
THE GRAND DUKE OF THORTONBURG WISHES TO ANNOUNCE THE SHOCKING ENGAGEMENT OF PRINCE ROLAND TO PRINCESS LILLIAN MONTAGUE OF ROXBURY, DAUGHTER OF HIS SWORN ENEMY!

LET IT BE KNOWN that "spare heir" **Roland** masqueraded as a stable hand at the Montague keep (we're still curious why) and fell for Princess Lillian, herself masquerading as a commoner....

LET IT BE KNOWN that **Lillian**, who's been rather reclusive in recent years (some say she was betrayed by a gold-digging love), along with Roland, have helped to ease the feud between their families that has been ongoing for decades....

Now, if only Lillian's widower brother, Prince Damon, could marry and provide the heir his parents and countrymen so desperately demand!

Dear Reader,

March roars in in grand style at Silhouette Romance, as we continue to celebrate twenty years of publishing the best in contemporary category romance fiction. And the new millennium boasts several new miniseries and promotions... such as ROYALLY WED, a three-book spinoff of the cross-line series that concluded last month in Special Edition Arlene James launches the new limited series with A Royal Masquerade, featuring a romance between would-be enemies, in which appearances are definitely deceiving....

Susan Meier's adorable BREWSTER BABY BOOM series concludes this month with Oh, Babies! The last Brewster bachelor had best beware—but the warning may be too late! Karen Rose Smith graces the lineup with the story of a very pregnant single mom who finds Just the Man She Needed in her lonesome cowboy boarder whose plans had never included staying. The delightful Terry Essig will touch your heart and tickle your funny bone with The Baby Magnet, in which a hunky single dad discovers his toddler is more of an attraction than him—till he meets a woman who proves his ultimate distraction.

A confirmed bachelor finds himself the solution to the command: Callie, Get Your Groom as Julianna Morris unveils her new miniseries BRIDAL FEVER! And could love be What the Cowboy Prescribes... in Mary Starleigh's charming debut Romance novel?

Next month features a Joan Hohl/Kasey Michaels duet, and in coming months look for Diana Palmer, and much more. It's an exciting year for Silhouette Books, and we invite you to join the celebration!

Happy Reading!

Mary-Theresa Hussey
Senior Editor

Please address questions and book requests to:
Silhouette Reader Service
U.S.: 3010 Walden Ave., P.O. Box 1325, Buffalo, NY 14269
Canadian: P.O. Box 609, Fort Erie, Ont. L2A 5X3

A ROYAL MASQUERADE

Arlene James

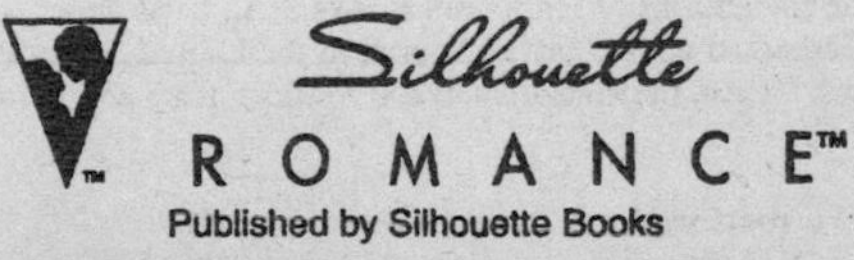

Published by Silhouette Books
America's Publisher of Contemporary Romance

Special thanks and acknowledgment are given to Arlene James for her contribution to the Royally Wed series.

SILHOUETTE BOOKS

ISBN 0-373-19432-3

A ROYAL MASQUERADE

This edition published by arrangement with Harlequin Books S.A.

Visit us at www.romance.net

Printed in U.S.A.

Books by Arlene James

Silhouette Romance

City Girl #141
No Easy Conquest #235
Two of a Kind #253
A Meeting of Hearts #327
An Obvious Virtue #384
Now or Never #404
Reason Enough #421
The Right Moves #446
Strange Bedfellows #471
The Private Garden #495
The Boy Next Door #518
Under a Desert Sky #559
A Delicate Balance #578
The Discerning Heart #614
Dream of a Lifetime #661
Finally Home #687
A Perfect Gentleman #705
Family Man #728
A Man of His Word #770
Tough Guy #806
Gold Digger #830
Palace City Prince #866
*The Perfect Wedding #962
*An Old-Fashioned Love #968
*A Wife Worth Waiting For #974
Mail-Order Brood #1024
*The Rogue Who Came To Stay #1061
*Most Wanted Dad #1144
Desperately Seeking Daddy #1186
*Falling for a Father of Four #1295
A Bride To Honor #1330
Mr. Right Next Door #1352
Glass Slipper Bride #1379
A Royal Masquerade #1432

*This Side of Heaven

Silhouette Special Edition

A Rumor of Love #664
Husband in the Making #776
With Baby in Mind #869
Child of Her Heart #964
The Knight, the Waitress
and the Toddler #1131
Every Cowgirl's Dream #1195
Marrying an Older Man #1235
Baby Boy Blessed #1285

Silhouette Books

Fortune's Children
Single with Children

The Fortunes of Texas
Corporate Daddy

ARLENE JAMES

grew up in Oklahoma and has lived all over the South. In 1976 she married "the most romantic man in the world." The author enjoys traveling with her husband, but writing has always been her chief pastime.

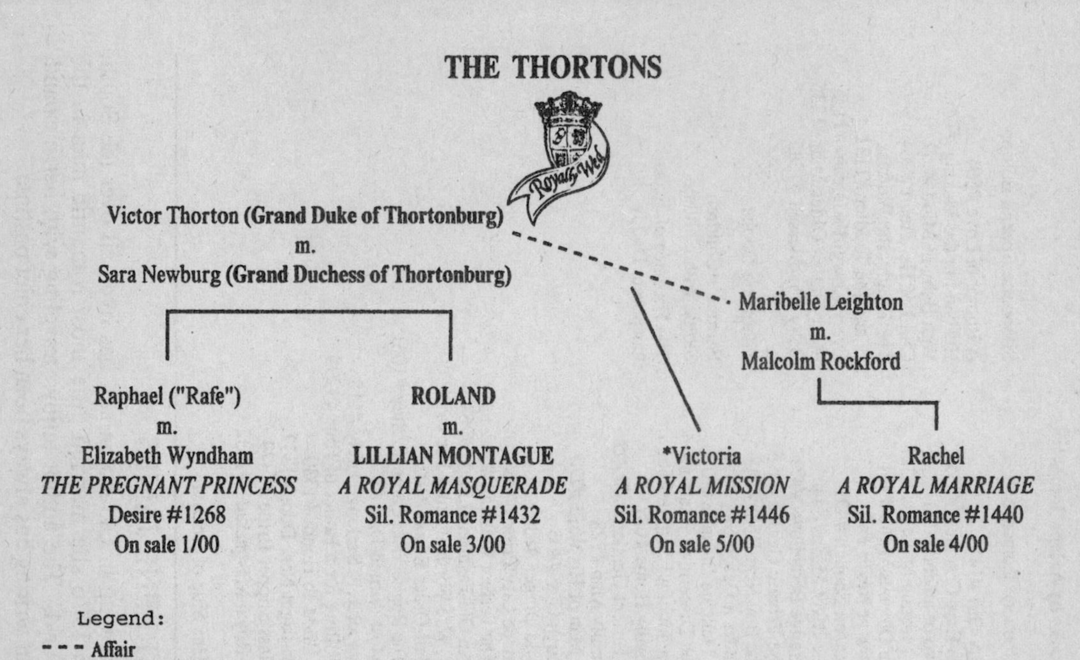
THE THORTONS
Royally Wed
Victor Thorton (Grand Duke of Thortonburg)
m.
Sara Newburg (Grand Duchess of Thortonburg)
Maribelle Leighton
m.
Malcolm Rockford
Raphael ("Rafe")
m.
Elizabeth Wyndham
THE PREGNANT PRINCESS
Desire #1268
On sale 1/00
ROLAND
m.
LILLIAN MONTAGUE
A ROYAL MASQUERADE
Sil. Romance #1432
On sale 3/00
*Victoria
A ROYAL MISSION
Sil. Romance #1446
On sale 5/00
Rachel
A ROYAL MARRIAGE
Sil. Romance #1440
On sale 4/00
Legend:
- - - Affair
* Child of Affair

Chapter One

The obsequious little man in state dress, complete with the sash of office, made yet another bow and droned on. "We of Wynborough understand, of course, and most assuredly admire the rich maritime history of our trusted and revered ally Thortonburg."

"Our piratical history, you mean," Roland Thorton interrupted with droll impatience, secretly amused to see the little man jerk and grapple with his composure.

"Oh, no, Your Highness. Never!" The man gasped, as if shocked to his core.

"Come now," Roland said, frowning and drumming his fingertips on the ornate arms of his chair in a show of regal boredom while delightedly baiting the snobbish little twit. "We Thortons are not ashamed of our forebears. Pirates they were, fierce and unscrupulous, and they kept our marvelous isle afloat with their ill-gotten gains. Our current shipping concerns are but a pale, distant image of those magnificent marauders of our past. We are pirates of banking and horseflesh, oil and tourism now. And it is the same with our smaller neighbor of Roxbury, though I have little doubt that Prince Charles would deny it. Pirates we were, sir, battling for the same plunder. Now we are but dignified and proper purveyors of goods, vying for the same contract year after year with your honorable King Phillip for no good reason except that it is tradition. So, who shall it be? Does my father, the Grand Duke of Thortonburg, or Prince Charles Montague of Roxbury win this year's shipping contract with Wynborough?"

The little man gulped and dug a finger beneath the tight, starched collar of his shirt, bobbing from the waist in that perpetual bow. "As to that, my lord Roland, His Majesty King Phillip bears the highest regard for Thortonburg and all its interests."

"I should hope so," Roland drawled. "He saw his daughter married to Thortonburg's heir apparent, after all." He leaned forward suddenly, skewering the statesman with a pointed glare. "I should think that as my brother Raphael is son-in-law to your king, special consideration might be given to us. Even now Princess Elizabeth awaits the birth of a child who will further both royal lines." Actually, it was his father, the Grand Duke, who thought special consideration should be given, despite the fact that Rafe refused to ask his wife to intervene on Thortonburg's behalf. Roland had his personal doubts, which his father, as usual, chose to ignore.

Wynborough's Deputy Minister of Trade drew himself up to his official best and finally—finally—approached the heart of the matter. Roland gritted his teeth, suspecting what was coming and dreading what would follow.

"There, Prince Roland, you have hit squarely upon the problem. Surely you understand that His Highness must avoid all semblance of favoritism. He means to rule justly, you see."

Impatiently, Roland crossed his legs and flicked lint from the trousers of his ceremonial costume. "Yes, yes. Out with it, if you please, while I am still young. Do we or do we not have the contract?"

The minister pursed his lips, abandoned diplomacy and answered baldly, "Not."

Roland slumped, half in relief, half in regret and wholly in exhaustion. The celebration of King Phillip's twenty-year reign as monarch of Wynborough continued unabated, despite the fact that numerous business meetings such as this one were taking place all over Wyndham Castle. In truth, it was the business that brought Roland to Wynborough. Although his presence as a member of the royal family of Thortonburg was required and expected, he had little patience with pomp and circumstance, which, to his mind, was to be endured rather than enjoyed and then only when absolutely necessary. Twenty-six years of training, however, immediately had him straightening his spine again. Squaring his shoulders, he gave his head that regal tip.

"You are telling me that we have lost the contract precisely because my brother has married a royal princess of Wynborough. Is that correct?"

The bureaucrat bowed his head. "I regret to say that it is."

It was just as Roland had suspected. His father would not be pleased, and though it was Raphael's connections that had cost them the contract, it was he, Roland, who would bear the blame. He, after all, had been running Thorton Shipping while his brother had been establishing a construction business in America. Not that he blamed Rafe. Indeed, he would have gladly joined him. The trappings of royalty, he knew only too well, were often as much trap as bother. But someone had to tend the till. Raphael could not suspect how delighted Roland was to have his older brother home and involving himself in the running of the country. Or perhaps he did. Rafe was no one's fool, and love seemed to have made him unexpectedly insightful. *That* was one complication Roland was determined to avoid.

Love was well enough when it brought his brother home to his duty, but Roland intended to simplify his own life now. It was time to see to his own future, and he had in mind a certain lush little island nestled neatly between Thortonburg and Roxbury. A Thortonburg principality, it had been suggested for development because of its pristine beaches, but Roland had quietly quashed that idea, envisioning instead a horse ranch and stud farm of unparalleled prominence. To that end, he had begun acquiring the finest stock to be had in all of Europe and was even now arranging the transport of an Irish thoroughbred of supreme line and conformation, a most spirited beast as fast as the wind and black as the night. Roland hadn't decided on a name for him yet. Something piratical perhaps.

The minister droned on, assuring Roland that Thorton Shipping enjoyed the favor of the Wyndhams and that only circumstance had cost them the contract. He would have said the same things to Montague had the Thortons secured the contract instead. Only the fact that he was a guest at Wynborough prevented Roland from simply getting up and walking out of the opulent chamber. It was with relief and bemusement, then, that he watched a concealed door open in the wainscoting next to the fireplace and a costumed footman appear.

The Deputy Minister scowled at the interruption, but the footman could not be outdone in magisterial hauteur. Back and shoulders straight, he looked down his nose into nothingness and announced pompously, "Begging your pardon, Deputy Minister, I have an urgent personal message for Prince Roland of Thortonburg."

The Deputy Minister flattened his lips together, obviously disgruntled to have his official business curtailed before all the appropriate niceties were performed and he was given his due by the prince of Thortonburg. Nevertheless, protocol demanded that he cease and desist.

Roland was both thrilled and wary. He welcomed the opportunity to be rid of the minister at the very same moment that he prepared himself for yet another thankless assignment. Rising, he concluded his business with the minister, curtly thanking the silly man for his time. Silently, the deputy backed away, bowing and scrambling as Roland strode straight for the footman. Bending his head, he allowed the footman to whisper into his ear.

"The Grand Duke and Duchess of Thortonburg request your immediate audience, sir. I've been asked to escort you to a private apartment via the quickest route."

Roland straightened and lifted an imperious brow. The quickest route, was it? Immediacy was ever one of his father's requirements, but this summons contained the flavor of true haste. The mention of his mother made it a family matter. Curious, but convenient. His mother's presence would temper the Grand Duke's outburst when Roland told him that his coveted shipping contract was to be denied him for another year. It would be fuel to the fire, however, of the ongoing feud between the Thortons and the Montagues of Roxbury. Personally, Roland found the whole thing asinine. He understood that once the shipping contract had meant the difference between prosperity in the coming year or hard times for the common people, but that had ceased to be a real issue before the Second World War. These days, it was more a matter of ego, a personal vendetta waged by minions on behalf of his father and Prince Charles of Roxbury—and Roland was, unfortunately, one of those minions. Ah, well, best get the thing behind him for another year.

Tugging at the cuffs of a black cutaway coat of a costume that was as much tuxedo as uniform, Roland nodded at the footman. "Lead on, then."

The footman slid a triumphant look at the thwarted deputy, putting that man firmly in his place, and executed a neat pivot on the heel of one foot, plumes bobbing from his ridiculous headdress. "This way, Your Highness, if you please." With that he stepped into the opening in the wall and led Roland through a maze of winding, identical passageways and staircases. To Roland's bemused amazement, they stepped through yet another wall and into the hallway just outside the opulent apartments assigned to his family. The footman stepped up to the door and rapped it smartly with his gloved knuckles.

Roland pushed past him to open the door and walk into the large salon joining his assigned rooms with those of his parents. He was not surprised to find that he was the last to arrive, since he naturally would have been the last summoned. The Grand Duke lived and breathed protocol, hence the heir would always be called upon before the "spare." Fortunately for Roland, he was genuinely fond of his elder brother and did not covet his birthright in the least. It was difficult, however, to constantly feel the lack of his father's approval, especially since Raphael was the one who had escaped to America all those years, leaving Roland behind to deal with his royal responsibilities and autocratic parent alone. Now that Rafe had returned to the fold and established a truce with their father, Roland was beginning to scent escape. He truly hoped that Rafe and Elizabeth would eventually settle permanently in Thortonburg and take up the reins of power.

Roland smiled and nodded to his mother, then strolled

over to test the waters by delivering a companionable whack to his brother's shoulder. Rafe slid a small, taut smile at him, his gaze trained warily on their father. Something serious was afoot then, and not even Rafe knew what it was all about yet. Roland turned his attention to the Grand Duke and was surprised to find one-time Wynborough royal bodyguard Lance Grayson standing at his father's back. Lance was a member of the Thortonburg security team now, head of the Investigative Division.

Roland felt a chill of premonition. His training served him well, however, and he kept the worrisome emotion firmly masked.

"Your timing is impeccable, Father. I had just gotten to the heart of the matter with that little cockroach of a deputy minister."

Victor, Grand Duke of Thortonburg, removed his elbow from the mantle of a cold marble fireplace and clasped his hands behind his back, lifting his chin imperiously. He was a tall, big man, long-limbed and thick in the chest with silver hair and sharp blue eyes, every inch the regent. "And?"

Roland shook his head, his dread carefully concealed. "King Phillip does not want to appear to be playing favorites. The contract goes to Roxbury again this year."

Victor turned away in disgust. Something akin to shock settled over Roland as he realized that his father wasn't going to explode—yet. Raphael sighed loudly and commented, "So you were right, Roland. Good call. Unfortunately."

Roland's mouth quirked in a grateful smile. That sensitivity of Rafe's was working overtime.

"Maybe it's connected," Victor said suddenly, turning to Lance Grayson.

Grayson looked down at something in his hands and

shrugged. "I suppose it's possible, but at this point, no one can say."

Sara Thorton spoke up from her place on the small, French provincial sofa where she sat with her tiny hands folded in her lap, her back ramrod straight, her soft platinum gray hair swept into a classic roll. "Isn't it time we were all told what has happened? Frankly, you're frightening me, Victor."

Victor Thorton sighed, and for the first time in memory, Roland saw his father as tired and uncertain. "I fear you're all going to be terribly shocked," he said in an oddly strained voice, "as I am myself. A man's mistakes often rise up to devour him, and, dammit, I know no other way to fight this thing than to simply take it by the throat. You might as well hear for yourselves, then." Straightening, he once more clasped his hands behind his back and nodded at Lance Grayson, who cleared his throat, lifted a paper, unfolded it and began to read.

"'To the Grand Duke of Thortonburg. I have your daughter.'"

The duchess gasped. Like Roland, Raphael stood in frozen shock for a moment, but then he chuckled. "What kind of joke is this?"

Roland, however, was looking at their father, who seemed to have aged several years in the past few moments. "Doesn't sound like a joke to me," he murmured.

"What else could it be?" his mother exclaimed. "We don't have a daughter!"

"*You* don't have a daughter," Victor ground out, turning away guiltily.

"Victor?" Sara said, her voice wobbling high.

"Could we please take this one step at a time?" Victor growled. "Let us at least get through the note. Grayson, if you please."

The security agent cast a bland look around the room and began again. "'To the Grand Duke of Thortonburg. I have your daughter. Before you throw her life away as you did that of her mother, Maribelle, take a good look at the enclosed photograph. No doubt you'll agree that the family resemblance is pronounced. Add to this the existence of a raspberry birthmark in the shape of a teardrop and identification is a certainty.'"

Roland traded looks with his brother. The birthmark was a closely guarded family secret, a hedge against impostors, a secret held by generations of Thortons—until now. Grayson went on reading.

"'The life of an innocent young woman may mean nothing to you, but have no doubt that the world will know your dirty secrets if you fail to follow my future instructions to the letter. Do nothing—contact no agency—until then.' And it's signed, 'The Justicier.'"

"What does it mean?" Sara asked after a moment fraught with heavy silence.

Before taking it upon himself to answer, Lance Grayson glanced at the Grand Duke, who turned to lean both arms against the mantlepiece, presenting his bowed back to the room. Grayson folded his hands, feet braced wide apart in a familiar stance. "Obviously the kidnapper considers him or herself the dispenser of justice, which I expect takes a monetary form. Otherwise, he or she would merely leak this young woman's existence to the press and be done with it."

"You're saying this person, this alleged Thorton daughter, exists," Rafe stated unequivocally.

Lance Grayson said nothing to that, merely looked pointedly at the Grand Duke. Victor slowly straightened, tugging at the hem of his eggshell-white, military-style ceremonial coat. Turning, he extracted something from a pocket, a photograph. Looking down at it, he seemed to struggle for a moment. When he looked up again, he had eyes only for his wife.

"It only happened once," he said stiffly, "long ago, and her name was, indeed, Maribelle."

Sara lifted a trembling hand to her mouth. In that moment, she appeared as something less than the Grand Duchess of Thortonburg. Instead, she looked, for all the world, like every loving wife facing her worst moment of betrayal. Roland felt his hands curl into fists, but by sheer habit the anger that his father all too often aroused in him remained carefully, tightly controlled. Rafe glanced his way before stepping forward to address their father.

"You're telling us that we have a sister?"

"I'm telling you that it's possible, even probable." With that, Victor handed over the photograph. Rafe stepped close to Roland and lifted the small, camera-developed snapshot. The resemblance was unmistakable. Dark hair, blue eyes, patrician features in an oval face. She was smiling, the photo obviously having been taken in an unguarded moment. Roland felt his heart lurch. His sister. A surge of fierce protectiveness surprised him.

"She looks to be about my age," he said.

"A year older, I would expect," Victor confirmed. He turned to his wife defensively. "It happened over twenty-seven years ago. We married for duty, Sara, but love came later, didn't it?"

She nodded, dabbing at the corners of her eyes with a linen handkerchief that had appeared from somewhere. "I remember," she said. "We were...estranged."

"Yes. It was so hard to understand and admit that the marriage of duty into which we had entered had become so very...emotional."

"I suppose it was my fault," she said, looking up at him

through her tears. "I changed the rules on you. I was the one who wanted, needed, more."

The duke bowed his head momentarily and cleared his throat before saying, "That's not entirely true. I just didn't know how to deal with changes in my own feelings. I...ran away."

"To Glenshire," Sara added, remembering, "the old hunting lodge."

"I met Maribelle there in Glenshire," he rasped. "I thought that an affair with her would restore my perspective, and it did, only not in the way I expected. She was dear and lovely and lonely, I think, and we both knew that I would never stay with her. When I ended it, I knew that the only woman I would ever again want was waiting for me at home."

Sara chuckled tearfully. "You pursued me—courted me, really—after eight years of marriage. I didn't care why. Then."

"I won't ask you to forgive me," Victor said stiffly, "only to support my efforts in this. Whatever I've done, the girl is innocent."

For a long moment, Sara Thorton said nothing, merely stared sadly at her husband, but then she lifted her hand to her face and skimmed away her tears. "Roland came after that reconciliation. You've given me two wonderful sons, one out of duty and one out of love. But I always wanted a daughter, and you gave her to another woman."

Victor pursed his lips, obviously fighting his own emotions. "I didn't want to hurt you," he said finally. "I wanted to spare you this knowledge. I wanted to spare us both this moment. I never knew about the child, but if she's mine, and it seems that she is, I must find her."

"It could still be an elaborate hoax," Grayson pointed out, his even tone not quite hiding his discomfort at witnessing such a personal exchange. "The girl may not be a Thorton at all. We have to find out what has become of this Maribelle and whether or not she even has a daughter."

Sara briskly dried her eyes. "Yes, yes, you're right, of course, Mr. Grayson. That should be our first step."

Roland glanced down at the photo that he had taken from his brother's hand. His gut told him that this was no hoax, but they had to be sure. Meanwhile, they had to consider what to do next. The trouble was that his own mind was whirling. *You gave me two wonderful sons, one out of duty and one out of love.* Roland couldn't help wondering if his brother had picked up on that statement. Personally, he was having a little trouble thinking of himself as the love child in the equation.

"Could I see that, please, Roland?"

The sound of his mother's voice brought his gaze up from the face in the photo. He slid a look at his father, not really contemplating withholding the snapshot but wanting the duke's full acquiescence anyway. Victor walked across the room, his hand held out for the photograph. Roland slid the snapshot into his father's hand and waited with Raphael to take in his mother's response. Victor delivered the photo gently and stood awaiting his wife's reaction. Sara cupped the likeness in her hand and studied it for a long while.

"She's very beautiful," the duchess said at last, "and every inch a Thorton." She looked up at the assembled group and asked, "Who could do this, kidnap an innocent young woman and hold her for ransom?"

The atmosphere in the room changed somehow, coalesced with a fresh, strong sense of purpose. They were banded together as a family in that moment, united in support of their own, as they never had been before. His mother might not have forgiven her husband's long-ago infidelity, but she had accepted his secret daughter as one of the family. Roland felt an almost overwhelming sense of pride. Victor clasped both hands behind his back and lifted his chin regally.

"Enemies are the price of ruling," he said. "We are not without ours."

Grayson shrugged. "I would categorize most as rivals, rather than true enemies."

"Rivals and enemies," Victor mused, eyes narrowing. "Charles Montague." He turned his head to impale his youngest son with a sharp gaze. "The shipping contract. You met privately with the Deputy Minister this morning. The ransom note had already been delivered."

Roland nodded, thinking it through. "The note doesn't mention money, only that you are to follow instructions. It could be that, not knowing the matter is already resolved, Charles Montague means to force you to withdraw your bid. But why? He's never gone to such lengths before."

Victor shook his head. "I was so sure Raphael's marriage to Elizabeth would weigh in our favor." He looked up suddenly. "And who is to say that Montague wouldn't assume the same? It's reasonable that a son-in-law's interests would supercede diplomatic ones in this case. Montague might have assumed that he needed an upper hand in the negotiations. He could have discovered the girl accidentally and had her kidnapped in an effort to force us to back out of negotiations."

Raphael shook his head. "The contract's just not that important."

"Isn't it?" Victor demanded. "Just what is honor worth in this world then?"

Roland didn't agree that the shipping contract was a matter of honor, but he saw no reason to argue the point. What mattered was that Charles Montague seemed to think the same way that Victor did about the issue. Roland stroked his chin thoughtfully. "I don't know. It's possible. After all, no one expected the decision to be made so quickly, and the Deputy Minister did preface all his remarks with the statement that King Phillip wanted to inform us of his decision first out of familial consideration."

Rafe nodded, conceding the point. "That makes sense. Montague still might not know that Phillip has made his decision."

"The note was delivered before last night's celebrations," Grayson pointed out. "The Wyndhams' social secretary discovered it and gave it directly to the Grand Duke."

"Montague couldn't have known that he'd won the contract then," Roland said.

"My marriage to Elizabeth might have led him to believe that Thortonburg had the edge and pushed him into action," Rafe mused.

"It must be Montague!" Victor exclaimed, launching to his feet.

"It does bear investigating," Grayson said carefully, "but we have to play this one close to the vest. The fewer who know what is going on the better."

Suddenly Roland knew exactly who could accomplish the task of investigating the Montagues. He had played his role in the Thortonburg ruling family in relative obscurity. Never the heir, he was ignored by most in the upper echelons of government. He'd made sure to keep himself out of the papers and off the news. Moreover, the enmity between the Montagues and the Thortons had insured that a certain distance was kept by the families.

"We need someone inside Roxbury," Grayson continued, "someone who can get close to the Montagues, someone utterly trustworthy who knows what he's about and can make himself invisible."

Victor nodded and asked of Grayson, "Do you have anyone in mind?"

Lance Grayson looked to Roland, saying, "Not exactly, but I think your son might."

Victor looked at Roland in surprise. "Who?"

Roland, coldly purposeful, kept his smile tight and said, "Me."

For an instant, just an instant, he expected praise to fall from his father's lips, but in the end Victor reverted to type and snapped, "Don't be absurd. A son of the royal house of Thortonburg?"

"Now, wait a minute," Rafe said, raising his voice slightly. "Who could be more trustworthy?"

"And Roland has kept a low profile," Grayson pointed out.

"The only Montague who's ever laid eyes on me, except at a very great distance, is Damon, and the last time was years ago."

"But the Thortons are very distinctive, dear," Sara pointed out.

"In ceremonial dress, yes, but in jeans, boots and a cowboy hat, no one in Roxbury will know me from Adam."

"You expect to just walk right into the manor and start asking questions?" Victor demanded.

Roland bit back an irate retort. He'd learned long ago that he got farther with his autocratic parent if he applied cold logic. "I expect to find a job somewhere on the place, possibly the stables. I've no doubt the Montagues have as much difficulty finding good help in that area as we do."

Victor gave him a blank look, and Roland smiled inwardly. Victor was the last person to know about the difficulties of finding good help. He had others to take care of those small details of everyday life for him—and Roland was one of those *others,* especially when it came to an area of such intense personal interest for him as his horses.

Grayson was nodding. "It might work. It just might work, especially if you put in your first appearance in Roxbury before the festivities end."

Rafe slapped Roland on the back. "Grayson is right. No one would expect a self-respecting royal to leave the party before it's over."

"You'll be missed," Sara worried aloud.

Roland smirked. "I haven't been so far, Mother, not even by you, it would seem."

"But you've been in attendance at every..." She broke off as Roland shook his head. "But you agreed..." When he shook his head again, she collapsed back against the sofa cushions in disgusted defeat.

"I agreed to accompany you and Father here to the festivities. I didn't agree to take part in them myself."

"But what have you been doing with yourself?" Victor demanded.

Raphael coughed to stifle a chuckle and said, "He's been in the stables, I would imagine."

Roland grinned at his astute brother. "Your father-in-law hasn't anything to compare with Thorton stock, despite the size of his stable."

Rafe clapped an arm around Roland's shoulders. "I say Roland gets this assignment."

"I agree," Grayson seconded.

Victor studied Roland for a moment, then nodded his head sharply. "All right. Roland is our man in Roxbury. Grayson investigates Maribelle and coordinates the operation."

"What about me?" Rafe asked.

Victor sighed. "You and I will quietly set about freeing up some of our assets. Whoever the blackguard is behind this, he'll be asking for money, if only to throw us off the track and hide his real identity now that the shipping contract is settled. If all else fails, we'll pay his bloody ransom."

"And bring that poor girl home," Sara added firmly.

The men shared a look among themselves, agreeing in silence not to mention the very real possibility to Sara that, even with the ransom in hand, the kidnapper might still be willing to rid him or herself of witnesses, most especially the victim. But they weren't about to let that happen, not to a Thorton.

"Don't worry, my lady," Grayson said. "Whoever she is, we'll get to the bottom of this."

"If she's our sister," Raphael began.

"We'll bring her home," Roland added.

"Where she belongs," Victor finished implacably.

For the first time, it seemed, the Thorton men were of one mind and one purpose. Shipping contracts and ceremony be damned. This was family. This was real. And Roland sensed that it was going to change them all.

Chapter Two

Roland stood atop a grassy knoll in the soft light of this spring morning, listening to the sound of his horse cropping the rich fodder beside him, and staring at the centuries-old seat of the Montague family. The island nation of Roxbury itself was smaller than its neighbors, but the house in the distance was, in fact, nothing short of a castle. Built in the Austrian style, it was a rambling confection spun of salt-white stone, complete with turrets and an apron wall that was once part of significant fortifications. The outer wall with its cannon platforms had been torn down long ago, leaving a nearly unobstructed view of the castle itself from this vantage point.

Roland shook his head. The castle was a beautiful sight, but he was not concerned with aesthetics. It was the sheer size of the place, the number of rooms that troubled him. A hostage could be hidden in any of several dozen places within those walls, but instinct told him that none was.

In the three days he had been here, he'd asked for and received an "insider's" tour of the castle from an accommodating maid, and he had carefully, casually questioned the staff about the possibility of an incognito guest on the premises. His questions had aroused no apparent interest or discomfort. If his sister was being held by the Montagues, it was not, apparently, here.

His sister. Roland marveled that his stiff, autocratic, duty-bound father had, for once in his life, surrendered to the temptations of normal human frailty. He marveled at the growing sense of affiliation and affection that he himself felt for a woman he had never met, whose very existence had been unknown to him until a few short days ago. It was as if he knew her on some elemental level, as if she had always been there, a part of him that he had only recently identified. And he was worried for her. Was she safe? Frightened? Lonely? Did she know that someone, anyone, cared? Had she any hope of rescue?

A movement in the outer yard caught his eye, and he focused there for a moment. Someone had come—several someones by the looks of things. A number of cars were parked in the carriage niches built into the apron wall. He had heard nothing from his room atop the stables last night, but the party must have arrived then. He'd been up with the dawn, and no one had arrived since then. Indeed, the household was only beginning to awaken now. After resetting his worn, dingy gray felt cowboy hat so that it rode lower on his forehead, he mounted the big bay gelding he'd chosen to exercise that morning and kicked into a gallop. As Rollie, newly hired stablehand and ostler, his absence would be noted soon.

He walked the bay into the stable some ten minutes later to find Jock Browning, the stable master, hitching his suspenders over his shoulder with one hand and gesturing to a pair of stirrup boys with a buttered croissant held in the other. A short, bow-legged man in his fifties with wild,

graying brown hair and dark-brown eyes, Jock was a true horseman, and he had claimed to recognize a kindred spirit in Rollie Thomas, stable hand. Roland couldn't help wondering if he'd feel the same way about Roland George Albert Thomas Thorton of the royal house of Thortonburg.
Jock turned at the sound of Roland's mount on the cobblestones and called, "We've a busy morning here, boyo. Unless he's lathered, leave that one saddled in the near stall and come give a hand."

Roland led the bay inside the stall and looped the reins around the holding cleat, then produced an apple core from his pocket, a remnant of his own meager breakfast, as a treat. With the horse munching contentedly, he went out to receive his working orders.

"What's up, Jock?"

"Eh, the prince and princess arrived last night with a pack of good-timers in tow, and Prince Damon sent word that they'd be riding early this morning, fifteen to twenty of them."

Roland whistled, suitably impressed, he hoped, for Jock's satisfaction. "That'll take just about every head of stock on hand."

Jock nodded and bit off a huge chunk of his croissant. After chewing energetically for a few moments, Jock said, "We'll saddle 'em all 'cept the palomino, the blood bay and the dun stallion."

Roland nodded. The pale-golden horse with the ivory mane and tail was only newly broken to the saddle. An animal of uncertain temperament, the sleek mare had not yet been given a name, a privilege meant for Princess Lillian, daughter of the house, though it was said she never actually rode. Roland had worked with the animal for a few minutes the day before and judged the mare to be a prime piece of horseflesh. With an almost regal bearing, the horse had the kind of fortitude and intelligence necessary for intense training, perhaps in steeplechase, though he'd yet to see the palomino truly put through its paces.

"Good thing I oiled all that tack yesterday," he said, hurrying to pull saddles and bridles from the tack room.

"Oh, Rollie," Jock called as the younger man moved away, "there's a huge pile of cook's croissants and a fresh pot of coffee in my office there. Snag what ye can afore ye start, eh?"

"Will do."

But he didn't. The merrymakers began pouring from the house only moments later, spirits and voices high. Roland recognized several of those in attendance, as well as the atmosphere. Sometimes celebrants, particularly those with little else to occupy them, were reluctant to let the festivities end. This lot had obviously followed the Montagues home in order to prolong the party after the week-long coronation celebration in Wynborough. Roland was careful to keep his hat pulled low and his manner deferential as he rigged one horse after another and threw riders into saddles with interlocked hands forming a mounting stirrup.

Damon Montague, to Roland's surprise, strode into the stable smiling and promptly saddled his own mount without waiting for help. He then cantered out alone, leaving behind a trio of petulant young women who had been hanging on him and obviously trying to fix his interest. Roland had to chuckle, knowing full well how Damon felt. Nothing put a determined woman on the hunt like a title and a fortune held by a single, eligible man. According to the servants' gossip, the Montague parents were matchmaking, throwing young women at their widowed son's head with all the finesse of a cannonade. Roland was thankful that his own status as younger son and his parents' apparent preoccupation with other matters had spared him a similar fate. The last thing he wanted at this point in his life was a wife.

More than an hour had passed before Roland was able to make his way to Jock's office and help himself to croissants and coffee. After finishing his cup, he picked up a final croissant and wandered back out into the stable. He just stood there, soaking in the atmosphere and enjoying the unabashed freedom of eating with his hands, when a cooing sound alerted him that he was not alone. Turning, he opened his mouth to take a bite of the flaky pastry, only to freeze at the sight of a pair of firm, well-rounded buttocks perched atop the gate to the palomino's stall.

The rump was definitely feminine, and clothed, not in tan, English-style riding breeches, but soft, faded denim. Roland tilted his head, taking in the slender legs and small, booted feet that were perched on a slat in the gate a good foot above the flagged floor. Whoever she was, she was small, but definitely not a child. No, that was a very womanly rump. She straightened suddenly, a bright, golden ponytail swinging between her shoulder blades as she teetered on the rail. Correction, that was a very womanly rump attached to a very womanly body with a tiny, nipped-in waist and slender, longish limbs, despite a diminutive stature.

Roland dropped his croissant and strode forward, catching her about the waist and setting her feet on the floor. She jerked around, eyes wide. Colors danced and sparked in those hazel eyes: blue, green, auburn, gold. They were framed by thick, dark-gold lashes and set off with sleek, matching brows that arched only slightly. Drawing back mentally, he widened his gaze to take in her whole face. Her forehead was high and wide, her nose aquiline and a tad more prominent than classical, her mouth a plump, rosy bow. The bone structure was strong, cheeks, jaw and chin definitely delineated. It was an intelligent face, amazingly unique, quite compelling and unusually lovely.

"What do you think you're doing?" she demanded.

"What do you think *you're* doing?" he countered. "That horse is not fully broken. It's off-limits."

She yanked her hand from beneath his and brought both free hands to her hips. His gaze dropped to her breasts. Yes, indeed, all woman.

"Who says?" she demanded.

He blinked, searching his mind for the proper reference for that question, and finally found it. "Jock says. He's—"

"The stable master, yes." She folded her arms, and a moment later he fought to bring his gaze up from her breasts again. "And who are you?"

He doffed his hat and made her an elaborate bow. "Rollie Thomas, new stable hand."

"Well, Mr. Thomas, this horse is a special interest of mine," she informed him coolly.

He grinned unrepentantly. "The name's Rollie. And who might you be?"

Those amazing eyes grew wide again, but in the next instant her hauteur softened. "I'm, er, Lily."

"Lily?" Why did that name sound familiar? "Well, Lily," he said smoothly, aware that his voice had dropped to a silky rumble, "I'm sure the palomino appreciates the sentiment. I should certainly like to be a special interest of yours. However, I've been given instructions that the horse is off-limits to everyone but the princess and—" Frowning, he stared at her. "Lily, that's the princess's name, isn't it?"

She smirked and rolled her eyes. "Hardly. Her name is *Lillian*." Imbued with all the importance of royalty, the name took on a whole new sound than the one in his head.

"Ah." Of course. Roland was royalty. Rollie was a stable hand. Likewise, Lillian was a princess. So what was

Lily? "I take it you're a guest. If you'd like a mount, I could saddle—"

"You take it wrong, Mr. Thomas. I am a resident."

His eyes narrowed, sensing something here, something that might turn out to be useful. "Is that so?"

"It is."

"Just, um, what is it that you do around here, if you don't mind my asking?"

She shrugged. "Ladies, um, that is, ladies' maids do whatever is required of them."

"Including hanging out in the stables?" he queried doubtfully, lifting his eyebrows.

She grinned. "Not just hanging out, working, and if I had my way, it'd be permanent. As it is, I can only get away so often, but thankfully Jock indulges me."

Roland leaned his forearms against the top rail of the gate and deliberately let his smile take on a flirtatious air. This assignment was suddenly having unforeseen bonuses. "Like the horses, do you?" he asked conversationally.

She mimicked his stance, stepping up on the bottom rung in order to do so. "Very much."

"Me, too. You must be pretty good if Jock lets you work the stock."

Her smile literally sparkled. "I like to think so. You must be pretty good yourself, for Jock to have hired you."

He chuckled. "The old man knows his stuff, doesn't he?"

"He's the best," she confirmed. The horse nickered and shifted in the stall. "What's the matter, baby?" she crooned. "Not getting enough attention? Come here. Come on. Come around here."

Roland watched, surprised, as the horse circled inside the box and ambled forward, coaxed by Lily's clucking tongue and cooing voice.

"That's my good girl," Lily sang, leaning forward to let the horse take her scent. She did not reach out her hand, not yet. "Whatever are we going to call you?" she murmured. "Sunshine? Goldie? Buttercup?"

Roland wrinkled his nose at the flowery names. "I thought Princess Lillian was to name her."

Lily shot him a sideways glance. "Hmm, she is." Lily leaned his way, confiding softly, "Between you and me, however, she'll need some help."

"Not too bright, is she?" he whispered, sidling closer.

Something flashed in her eyes, a spark of loyalty, perhaps. "Just...boring," she said finally.

"Unimaginative?" he prodded, liking the defensiveness that came into her posture. What good was a family retainer without some loyalty and affection for the family?

"Constrained," she corrected.

Now that he could understand. He nodded slowly. "Well, I hope she foregoes the pretty monikers. This lady deserves a strong name, something that reflects her spirit and value."

Lily considered that a moment, then turned her head to look at him. "What would you suggest?"

He shrugged, and the word just popped out of his mouth. "Doubloon." Inwardly, he winced. This pirate thing seemed to have taken him over lately. Lily, however, inclined her head.

"That's good. Doubloon. The gold Spanish treasure coin. I like that. I'll pass it on."

He smiled. "As long as you like it, that's satisfaction enough for me."

She measured him with a blatant look, then turned to hook an elbow over the top of the gate. "You're very forward."

"You're very beautiful," he shot back.

Her face pinched into a frown, but he caught the flare of pleasure in her eyes and dared her with his gaze to deny it. Suddenly she burst out with a laugh. "Well, it's not original as compliments go, but the delivery was excellent. I think it deserves at least a standard reply." She nodded her head. "Thank you."

"You're welcome."

He braced his elbows against the top of the gate, lifted his fists together and propped his chin atop them, waiting for her to choose the next step. She didn't disappoint him.

"What are you doing for the next little while?"

He straightened, kept his smile firmly locked away, and spread his hands. "Jock hasn't said yet. We were going to exercise the stock, but the riding party has taken care of that."

She hopped down off the gate, saying, "Let's put the Lady Doubloon through her paces. What do you say?"

He shouldn't. He knew without a doubt that it wasn't up to him to make such decisions, but he did it anyway. After all, she was a rich potential source of information, and if Jock "indulged" her interest in horses, she must be good. He lifted the latch on the gate. "Do you really think the princess will go for that name?"

Lily smiled. "I have a little influence."

"Oh?"

"I happen to know her personal maid."

Chuckling, he opened the gate. A rich source of information, indeed, and quite, quite lovely.

He was really quite handsome, Lily mused to herself. Though fairly tall—right at six feet, she judged—he did not overwhelm as her brother Damon did. Wiry but solid, he gave the impression of strength, both physically and mentally. And he didn't have the slightest clue who she really was, though there had been a moment when she feared he had tumbled onto the truth. Those in the stables who were aware of her identity were under strict orders to keep the information to themselves, so she had no fear that he would discover the truth that way. No doubt, it was unfair to mislead him. In fact, it was probably unwise, but she just couldn't help indulging herself a little. She grew so tired of the sycophants, the hangers-on who could never for a single instant forget who and what she was.

Sometimes she wanted to scream that she was a woman, a flesh-and-blood human being, but she doubted the humanity of those who surrounded her, those of her own social set. They simply wouldn't understand. Rollie, however, seemed sublimely human. What could it hurt if she indulged herself for a little while in something called "normalcy"?

Rollie led the newly christened Lady Doubloon into the working pen, and turned her loose. Lily bit back an order to secure the animal while Rollie went to the tack room for saddle, pads and bridle. He returned to hang the gear over the fence and rub his hands together eagerly.

"Ready?"

"Are you going to catch her again?"

"No." He shook his head. "That wouldn't serve any purpose. I'm going to make her come to me."

"You're what?"

He pushed his hat back and brought his hands to his lean hips. "Watch and learn, sweetheart. From over there by the fence, if you please."

Reminding herself that she was not the princess just now, Lily bit her tongue and did as she was told. Rollie went down on his haunches, hung his hands off his knees and puffed a blustering breath, bowing his head slightly so that he looked up at the horse from beneath his brow. His hair had seemed black in the shadows of the stable. Here in the sunlight Lily realized that the hair scraped back from his even hairline by the band of his hat was the color of dark chocolate.

She studied his face while he concentrated on the horse. Long and lean, with a squared-off chin and boxy jaw shadowed with a murky beard over dark golden skin, it was a distinctive face full of strong features. His mouth was wide and thin but neatly sculpted, his nose somewhat sharp with a slight bump just where it parted his straight, thick brows. The vibrant-blue eyes set deeply beneath those brows had proven both compelling and oddly unfathomable. She admired the breadth of his shoulders and the long, wiry length of his arms ending in big, squarish palms and long, tapering fingers. His booted feet were large; his legs long, powerful coils beneath him, despite his apparent ease as he crouched before the horse.

To Lily's surprise, the palomino suddenly swung her head wildly and pranced her front hooves. Rollie slid his arms to his sides, hunched his shoulders and bowed his head. After a moment, he slowly looked up again, a smile dancing in his deep-blue eyes. For some reason, Lily found herself holding her breath. Just when she'd decided that she was an idiot for doing so, the horse moved. Head bowed, it ambled over to where Rollie patiently waited and snuffled his hair, knocking off his hat. Rollie chuckled and lifted a hand to rub a flicking ear. For several delightful moments, the horse snuffled as Rollie rubbed his face and hands over its massive head and neck. Then slowly Rollie rose to his full height, careful to keep an arm lightly about the horse's neck.

Lady Doubloon tolerated this familiarity for some time before cantering off around the corral, playfully kicking up her heels and tossing her starlight-pale mane. She swept by

Rollie repeatedly, coming closer and closer. Other than retrieving his hat, Rollie stood his ground, letting the mare brush him as he laughingly avoided her hooves by shuffling his feet. Eventually, the horse cantered to a stop, hooves cutting grooves in the soft soil of the corral. Sides heaving, she blew into Rollie's palm. He ruffled her mane and hugged her, while Lily simply marveled.

Long minutes later, Rollie turned and walked calmly toward Lily and the tack spread out on the fence. Lady Doubloon fell into step beside him, for all the world like a friend out for a stroll.

"Get down," Rollie said to Lily. "Bow your head like I did."

Lily did as instructed, sinking down onto her haunches. After several moments, she felt the horse nosing, and then lipping, her ponytail. Rollie quietly instructed her, when to lift her hand, how to return Lady Doubloon's curious caresses. They were well known to each other, she and Lady Doubloon, and it didn't take long to establish what Lily could only call a firm friendship.

The saddle went on first, but was not cinched until Rollie deemed Lady Doubloon to be in agreement. When Lily pushed the bit between her teeth, the horse offered no resistance whatsoever.

"I'll take a seat first, if you don't mind," Rollie said, having adjusted the stirrups. Before Lily could answer, he swung up into the saddle, clearly not used to being gainsaid, despite the polite phrasing. He simply sat for a while, making himself comfortable in the saddle, before reaching for the reins, but even then he held the horse still. After some time, he got down again and began shortening the stirrups. "Your turn," he informed her.

Lily mimicked his behavior. She'd been on Lady Doubloon's back before, but the mare hadn't exactly been thrilled about it. This time, the horse seemed not only willing but eager.

"She's ready," Rollie said. "Take it slow and announce your intentions first."

"Announce my intentions?" Lily echoed.

He squinted up at her. "Just keep it simple. When you want to go, say so before you touch your heels to her flanks."

"I suppose you think she'll understand me," Lily quipped.

"She will eventually," he replied lightly, stationing himself at Lily's knee.

Considering all she had just seen, Lily was not inclined to argue. She picked up the reins and said, "Let's go, girl."

When she touched her heels to Doubloon's flanks, Rollie instantly stepped off. A split second later, the horse stepped off, too.

"Left," Lily announced, and just as she laid the rein against Lady Doubloon's neck, Rollie turned. The horse followed smoothly. This went on for some time, until the horse balked, at which point Rollie turned to caress her head, speaking softly.

"Now, now, in for a penny, in for a pound, my lady. We've begun work here, and if you're to become the splendid mount I know you can be, you must learn to obey loyally and promptly. Otherwise, you're just a pretty hobby, not even a good pet, and you're much too intelligent and beautiful for either." He looked up at Lily, then stepped back and folded his arms. "Again, with a bit more authority, if you please."

Lily repeated her command. To her surprise, Rollie stood still, but the horse performed instantly and flawlessly. When the animal balked again a few moments later, Rollie instructed Lily to "talk her into it." Lily leaned forward and spoke into the horse's ear while repeating her command action. Lady Doubloon flicked an ear, huffed, and reluctantly did as she was bidden. Rollie called a halt soon after.

Together, Lily and Rollie unsaddled and groomed the mare in her stall. All the while, Rollie heaped praise and affection on the animal. Finally, he treated the preening mare with a fistful of oats and a small piece of honeycomb, which he explained he liked to keep on hand for a special reward. When they left the stall, Lady Doubloon surprised Lily by trying to follow them. Rollie moved her back into the stall and closed the gate, saying, "Stay back. You've earned a rest, my love. I'll come round and check on you later, and the three of us will get together again soon. Goodbye for now." He rubbed the big golden head and gently tugged at the pale forelock.

Lily took her own leave in much the same way, murmuring, "Goodbye, Lady Doubloon, and thank you."

The horse huffed at them as they walked away.

"There's coffee in the office," Rollie said. "Have you time for a cup?"

"Yes, of course."

He slid her a quick look. "I suppose your mistress is out on the ride."

"Er, not exactly."

"No?" He pushed the office door back, allowing her to pass through the opening before him. "Just who is your lady?"

Lily wrinkled her nose and considered the lie carefully, finally deciding to get as close to the truth as possible. "I answer to the princess."

He lifted a brow at that and turned away to toss his hat onto the desk and fill two waxed paper cups with the strong, black brew left warming on an electric burner positioned on a rolling cart. Only at the last moment did he pause. "We have hot water if you prefer tea."

She shook her head, smiling. "I'm used to Jock's coffee."

He handed over the cups and leaned back against the battered desk while Lily took one of the equally battered chairs in front of it. A small leather sofa had been shoved up against the wall between a narrow bookcase and the door. A small barrel used as a footstool sat to one side. Dusty magazines and well-used books were piled together with various trophies and some detritus on the bookcase. A file cabinet in the corner behind the desk was overflowing with papers. A computer arranged on a narrow table against the wall blinked mistily from behind a plastic cover.

The coffee was bitter, but Lily did not complain. Rollie fairly chugged his, drinking it down in big gulps. She suspected that he probably drank too much of the stuff.

"That was amazing, what you did out there," she told him honestly. "Where did you learn such things?"

"America. It's a technique used in the northwest there."

"You've traveled then?"

He nodded. "Some. You?"

"Of course."

He smiled. "Ah, yes. A princess cannot be without her maid."

She smiled, too. "Just so."

He crossed his feet at the ankles and folded his arms. "Tell me, does the princess have any *unusual* guests just now?"

"Unusual?" Lily echoed, stiffening. "Whatever do you mean?"

He waved a hand negligently. "I was just wondering if the lot that came through here this morning are the usual faces seen around the princess and her brother, or if perhaps a more reticent guest might be in residence."

Lily stood up, feeling a distinct unease. "These are odd questions."

"Are they? I didn't realize. I'm just curious."

"About the guests?"

He shrugged negligently. "It pays to know such things. As a servant yourself, you must realize that certain types of knowledge are essential to anticipating your employer's needs—and those of her guests, of course."

She carried her cup to the one small, dusty window at the end of the room and pretended to gaze out at the lushly rolling landscape. "The lot that came through here this morning are the usual crew," she said lightly, "with the exception of a trio of young women in whom the prince's mother is trying to interest him."

Rollie chuckled. "Matchmaking mamas, one of the most formidable forces on earth. From what I saw this morning, she has her work cut out for her, though."

Lily turned to face the room again, smiling. "He calls them the unholy trinity."

"Does he?"

She nodded. "He doesn't want to be in love again. It's too painful for him, after losing his wife and child a little over a year ago."

Rollie sent her a strange look, something snapping in the mysterious depths of those blue eyes. "You sound as if you know Prince Damon rather well."

Oops. She glanced down at her cup, gathering her thoughts. "He and his sister are quite close. One absorbs certain knowledge just from being around."

"His mother doesn't seem to have absorbed that knowledge."

Lily wrinkled her nose. "She thinks that he'll get over

his loss more easily if he fixes his interest, and, of course, there is the succession to secure."

"Of course."

He was still looking at her oddly, that mysterious glint in his eye. "Tell me something," he said smoothly. "In your opinion, are the Montagues capable of acting, shall we say, unlawfully?"

She rocked back on her heels. "No! Why would you even ask such a thing?"

He shrugged. "I like to know who I'm working for, what to expect of them."

"I find your question insulting," she informed him with a tilt of her chin.

"Oh? Why is that?"

Why, indeed? She turned away, thinking quickly, and finally said, "I know the Montagues. I grew up around them. They can be fierce when one of their own is threatened."

"Ruthless?" he interjected.

She turned once more to meet his gaze levelly. "Yes, ruthless, when need be, but not malicious, never that."

He smiled, and something about it made her think that he didn't quite believe her. "The princess is fortunate to have you," he said silkily. "Such loyalty speaks well for both of you."

Lily lifted her chin a notch higher. "The princess needs no one to speak for her," she said smartly. "Now if you'll excuse me, I have to get back to the castle."

She circled the desk, placing her partially filled coffee cup in the trash can next to the cart. He shifted as she strode past him and shot out a hand, clamping it around her wrist.

"When will I see you again?" he asked softly.

She stared at his hand, stunned by the weight and heat of it, only belatedly realizing that his grip was gentle, unthreatening. Carefully, she rotated her wrist, freeing it. "I really couldn't say," she murmured, and swept from the room. She didn't slow down until she had cleared the tunneled archway through which she had entered the stables.

What a disturbing man he was, disturbing but compelling. And real. Perhaps more real than anyone she'd ever known before. How odd that was, to feel as if life was somehow more vibrant, more intense in him. He made her feel as if she had been hibernating, living half-awake. What he had done with that horse! She shivered and remembered the unsettling warmth of his hand. If she was wise, she would steer clear of Rollie Thomas. But for the first time in a very, very long time, she wasn't sure that the wisest course was the course she was going to take.

Chapter Three

Lily had scarcely cleared the door before Jock filled it. Wondering how much he'd overheard, Roland leaned back against the edge of the desk once more and folded his arms.

"Keeping yourself busy are you, boyo?" Jock said, holding his gaze level.

Roland shrugged. "Trying to. Where have you been? I expected—"

"What were you doing with Lily?" the old man demanded, and Roland had to tamp down his natural inclination to give rather than take orders. Reminding himself that he needed this job at least until the Montagues had been cleared as his sister's kidnappers, he swallowed down a sharp retort and took a deep breath.

"Just chatting. Why do you ask?"

"Lily's a special lass, due respect."

Roland bit back an angry answer and managed to keep his voice light and level. "Are you implying that I would treat the woman—any woman—with less than respect?"

"You tell me."

"If I have to do that, Jock, then you're not nearly as insightful as I've given you credit for being."

Jock pursed his lips, conceding nothing. "Has anyone ever told you that you speak like a college-educated man?"

"And you speak like an Irish curmudgeon," Roland returned smoothly.

"About Lily," Jock pressed.

Roland sighed inwardly. He was unused to explaining himself to anyone but his father. "We worked the palomino," he explained. "Lily assured me that she is allowed to deal with the animal."

"Aye. Go on."

"She's very good," Roland said.

"As if I didn't know," Jock retorted.

"She's determined to see the mare named Lady Doubloon. I warned her that the princess has the privilege of choosing, but as I said, Lily is determined."

"Determined?" Jock repeated, sounding mildly amused.

Roland nodded. "She seems to think she has some influence with her mistress."

"Oh, aye," Jock mumbled, rubbing his chin.

"Lily says the princess will listen to her," Roland went on, intent on putting Jock's suspicions to rest. "She says the princess needs help with such things, that she's 'boring' and 'constrained.'"

"Does she now?" Jock said, inclining his head as a small grin twisted his fat lips. "Constrained, aye. Boring, never."

"Do you think Lily can convince her to name the mare Lady Doubloon?"

"Without a doubt."

Roland nodded, having talked himself in a circle. A change of subject was in order. "Is the riding party returning?"

"Oh, aye, eventually, I dare say," was the reply. Jock folded his arms and looked up at him, not in the least intimidated by Roland's superior height and size. "Now why don't you tell me what you have planned for our Lily?"

Roland folded his own arms, mimicking the stable master's stance. "Planned?" He scoffed at the very notion. "I haven't planned anything for Lily. I only met her this morning."

"She's a bonny lass, is our Lily," Jock said warningly.

Roland chuckled mirthlessly. "So I noticed."

"Aye, and that's what troubles me."

Exasperation got the better of Roland. He brought his hands to his waist. "For pity's sake, Jock, I can't be the first man to have noticed that she's a beautiful woman."

"Not at all," Jock admitted. "But you're the first man she's noticed in many a day."

Roland's brows rose high. "Is that so?"

"Aye, that's so," Jock growled, "and I'm warning you now, lad, much as I like you, if you hurt our Lily, I'll come for you with hammer and tongs."

"You and who else, old man?" Roland challenged.

"You might be surprised," Jock said, and then he pulled himself up to his full height, such as it was. His round belly lifted, and his twill pants threatened to droop dangerously. Jock hitched them up with both hands. "Well, now that you've been warned, you'll go careful, I expect."

"Are you telling me to stay away from her?" Roland demanded, not at all liking the idea.

"Now would I do that?" Jock sounded shocked at the very notion. "I merely asked you to step easy, not to hurt her."

Roland opened his mouth—and closed it again. How was he supposed to argue with that? Demanding he not see Lily and asking him merely not to hurt her were two very different things, after all. Roland looked at his feet and cleared his throat. "I don't have any problem with that," he said.

"Well, now, I didn't really think you would," Jock replied.

Roland lifted a hand to the back of his neck. "Listen, what's going on with this Lily/Lillian thing? Since when do princesses share names with their maids?"

Jock rubbed his stubbled chin and said, "Naming a child after a princess is an act of respect, laddie, don't you think?"

"Mmm, I suppose so. I wonder if the princess doesn't mind, though."

"And why should she?"

"Frankly, I suspect the princess can't hold a light to Lily," Roland muttered.

"You think not?" Jock mused.

"Lily's not just beautiful, Jock. She has a gift with the horses."

"Aye, I know it well."

"What about the princess?"

Jock seemed to consider a moment. "Well, she considers herself something of a horsewoman, and she can sit a saddle as pretty as any, but I doubt we'll be seeing her much around here."

"Ah. Busy with royal duties, is she?"

"And keeps to herself when not," Jock said. "Lily, now, she's a regular. If them up at the big house would let her, she'd be working at your job."

Roland considered Lily's situation for a moment. He could relate. No doubt she chafed somewhat, living in the shadow of her princess, unable to do those things she really wanted to do, giving way always to the needs and wishes of her pampered, treasured, royal mistress. To a lesser degree, he had experienced those very things with his brother, but at least he was assured of his brother's affection, of having served the greater good. Lily could have no such assurance in her position. "She deserves better," he murmured.

"What's that?" Jock asked, leaning forward slightly.

Roland shook his head. "You were saying that Lily's the true horsewoman. I was just wondering how the princess measures up in the looks department."

"Well," Jock hedged, "Lily's the real beauty."

Jock's manner was enough to convince Roland that the princess was probably ugly as sin, so much so that the Montagues must keep her under lock and key, lest they scare off any potential suitors. "Ah," Roland said. "Just as I suspected."

Jock clapped his hands together. "Enough with the chatter. Let's you and me get them near stalls mucked out, boyo," Jock ordered. "Can't stand around gossiping like old maids all day, can we?"

Roland straightened, picked up his hat from the desk and slapped it onto his head. "Just hand me a shovel, man, and get out of my way."

Jock chuckled. "If it's a shovel you want, get it yourself then."

Saluting smartly, Roland strode from the room. If the smile lurking mischievously about Jock's mouth was too knowing and too wise, Roland failed to notice.

Lily tried to stay away, but the stables had always been her haven, and she was loath to let one cocky cowboy rob her of it. At least that was what she told herself as she changed into jeans and slipped out of the castle while her brother and their friends were watching a movie in the private screening room. No sooner had she entered the building than Jock appeared.

"I started to think you were hiding in that great house there, lass."

Jock had always been too insightful when it came to her, but she had always managed to put up a good front anyway. "Whatever are you going on about?" she said smartly. "I have guests, after all."

"Aye, which you do your best to avoid," he said. "You wouldn't be avoiding someone here now, would you?"

She did her best imitation of a princess looking down her nose at the impertinent help—to no avail whatsoever. "That's a silly thing to say. I just wasn't ready for a ride until now."

"Oh, o'course," Jock said all too knowingly. "Well, you won't mind doing for yourself, now will you?"

"Fine," Lily snapped, turning away to saunter down the aisle toward Lady Doubloon's stall. Do for herself. As if she had ever done less, she fumed. Reaching the stall, she paused to extract a folded napkin from her jacket pocket. Inside were several brussels sprouts. She plucked out a few and stashed the rest before climbing up on the bottom rail of the gate. "Hello, my sweet. I have a treat for you. What do you think of this?"

Lady Doubloon came to snuffle her palm and delicately lip up a brussels sprout. Lily listened to the horse crunch the raw sprout and offered another. One by one, she fed the hard green balls to the horse. Suddenly a familiar voice spoke.

"Ready to work?"

She hooked an elbow over the top of the gate and partly turned. A bridle flew at her. She caught it deftly and followed its flight path back to the grinning cowboy with the saddle and pads hoisted over one shoulder.

"Jock said you needed a little help."

"Oh, did he?"

"Surprised me, too," he admitted, "especially after the warning I got the other day."

"Warning?"

"Anyone who dares to bruise our darling Lily's heart will answer to the stable master."

Lily smiled to herself. "Jock's a little overprotective of me."

"I noticed. And I don't blame him. The question is, could your heart possibly be in danger from me, lovely Lily?"

"Only if you don't teach me your American technique for training horses," she quipped.

"In that case," he said, "we'd best get at it."

Laughing, they turned out Lady Doubloon together. She trotted around the corral, kicking up her heels in exuberance. "Such a beauty," Rollie murmured, and when Lily glanced in his direction, she saw that his gaze was on her rather than the horse. Instantly, her heart sped up, and she looked away again.

"It's official, by the way," she told him.

"What's that?" he asked, his brow furrowing beneath the band of his hat.

"Lady Doubloon. Princess Lillian has agreed to the name."

"Of course she did," Rollie said.

Alarmed, she backed up a step. "What's that supposed to mean?"

He smiled, his whole face lighting with it, and for a moment she saw the desire in his blue eyes. "A woman as beautiful as you is bound to get her way."

Lily relaxed, aware of a faint burn in her cheeks. "I hardly think Princess Lillian would be swayed by a pretty woman—or a handsome man, for that matter."

"She was obviously swayed by this one," he said, tapping her on the end of her nose with his finger before striding to the center of the corral. Lily breathed a sigh of relief. He didn't know. He didn't even suspect, apparently. As if signaled, Lady Doubloon cantered up and slid to a stop. Rollie threw the light pad and English saddle onto her back and spent some minutes lavishing the mare with affection before moving aside to fasten and tighten the girth.

Lily could only marvel. Both man and horse were remarkable; each was undeniably unique. And both liked her quite well without the slightest notion of her station. It wasn't the horse that made her heart beat like a triphammer, though. Determined to maintain her composure, Lily strolled up with the bridle and slipped the bit between the animal's teeth. When the headpiece was in place, Lady Doubloon demanded her due, snuffling Lily's face and butting her chest. Laughing, Lily hugged and scratched and stroked and petted until Lady Doubloon swung away.

"Want to go first?" Rollie asked, but Lily shook her head and backed toward the corral fence.

"I'll just watch for now."

"All right then."

Lily climbed up to sit on the top of the fence while Rollie began the instruction. Lady Doubloon balked from time to time, but Rollie patiently schooled her for about a half hour. Finally, he rode the mare over to the fence and got down. Leaving the mare standing obediently, he reached up and lifted Lily down from her high seat, his hands firm about her waist. Lily fought the urge to put her arms around his neck and lean into him.

"Your turn," he announced, climbing up onto the fence to sit in her place.

Lily shortened the stirrups, then glanced up at him. If she'd needed confirmation that he remained in the dark about her true identity, she received it when he simply stared back at her without offering to get down and give her a leg up. Rank, she mused silently, did have some privileges, but they were minor when compared with its demands. Grasping the saddle horn with one hand, she literally leapt and hauled herself upward at the same time, kicking her toe into the stirrup at the right moment.

"Bravo," Rollie complimented her as she swung into the saddle.

"You, sir," she drawled, "haven't seen anything yet."

She kicked Lady Doubloon into a canter, wheeling her away from the fence toward the center of the corral, leaving him behind laughing. The horse performed flawlessly. After a few minutes, Lily called to Rollie to open the gate. He got down off the fence without the slightest hesitation and did as she asked. Lily gave the mount her head, glorying as the palomino flew over the ground. Pulling the horse up and turning it into a trot was a challenge, but as soon as Lady Doubloon understood what was required, she complied readily enough. They cantered up to Rollie several minutes later and came to a halt. Lady Doubloon blew while Lily leaned forward and stroked her.

"She's wonderful. Amazing."

Rollie grinned and patted the horse's head. "We could ride out together tomorrow, if you like, really put her through her paces for the first time."

Lily wondered if she might not be making a big mistake, but in the end she couldn't seem to help herself. "I could bring a picnic lunch," she suggested.

"I'd like that," he said. "I'll have to ask Jock for the time."

"He won't say no," she promised, and Rollie grinned even wider, his blue eyes promising delights no other picnic had ever held.

* * *

Roland tickled her nose with the tip of a blade of grass. He'd been fighting the urge to kiss her all day. Worse, he'd been putting off asking her the very questions he'd brought her out here to ask, despite the fact that they were his only excuse for whiling away the hours with her like this. To Roland's surprise, Jock had given his permission readily enough when he'd asked for the time, but that did not eclipse his purpose in hiring on here in the first place. Roland reminded himself that the sister he had never met was depending on him.

"What do you know about the Montague holdings?" he asked idly as Lily slapped at the blade of grass. Her eyes popped open, and she rolled up into a sitting position, her legs stretched out straight in front of her.

"Why do you ask?"

He shrugged and looked away. "Just curious."

She tapped her feet together and seemed to consider. "What do you want to know?"

He shrugged again, blatantly lying. "Jock said something about a cottage somewhere, an old hunting box maybe."

She shook her head. "You must have misunderstood. The old hunting boxes fell into disrepair long ago and were destroyed for safety's sake. I'm unaware of any 'cottage' anywhere. There is an apartment in town, mostly for Damon's use, and several vacation homes are scattered around the world."

Roland narrowed his eyes. "Seems a pity, doesn't it, all those lovely homes standing vacant except for a few days a year."

Lily snorted inelegantly. "Prince Charles is most generous with such things. Some distant, less-fortunate member of the family always seems to be in residence. Let's see, Cousin Clifford is currently living in the Carribean house and has been since his last divorce." She leaned toward Roland conspiratorially. "Gossip around the castle has it that he's moved a pair of twins into the place with him. I think their names are Minna and Bette. I understand they're twenty-four, and Clifford is at least forty."

Roland chuckled. "Do tell."

Lily seemed to be warming to her subject. "Jolie is in the flat in Paris. She's the artistic sort, you know, haunts the museums with sketch pad and lover in tow. I'm told he's blind, which is convenient since he can't see how bad Jolie's drawings are."

Roland laughed. "You're naughty, to tell such things."

"Oh, but you haven't heard the best," she divulged with relish. "Harold has taken over the chalet in Switzerland, vowing to be the first Olympic downhill skier from Roxbury. They say he's let a commune take over the place and that they worship sex and the, quote/unquote, old gods."

"In that order no doubt," Roland quipped.

Lily waggled her shapely eyebrows. "No doubt."

They laughed together for a moment, and Roland resisted again the almost overwhelming need to push her down onto the blanket and make mad, passionate love to her—as if she would allow such a thing. He swallowed a lump that had suddenly appeared in his throat and forced himself to ask, "Is that it then? Only three vacation homes? I'd have thought a royal family would have vast holdings all over the world."

Lily shook her head. "It's just not cost-effective. Truthfully, I think the family maintains those places only so their relatives won't come here and live with them. There used to be an apartment in New York, but it was sold several years ago."

"Ah, well," Roland said lightly, "I guess being royalty just isn't everything it's cracked up to be."

"I think you could say that, yes," Lily agreed solemnly. Roland looked away.

He had no more reason to prolong the outing. He'd asked all the questions he dared, and staying here with her like this would be a clear invitation to trouble. He just didn't know how much longer he could keep his hands off her.

"We'd better get back," he whispered reluctantly. "I have a job to do."

Lily nodded and got to her feet. As she shook out the small blanket on which they'd eaten, Roland hoped that she would never guess that the job he meant was something other than mucking out stables.

She saw Rollie in town two afternoons later. Fortunately, when out in public, she often went incognito, big sunglasses, no make-up at all, her hair coiled up and covered by a scarf, a simple khaki skirt, canvas flats, white shirt and cardigan from the local discount chain. He was sitting alone at an outdoor table of an alfresco café, speaking on a cell phone. It was a serious conversation. She could tell from the expression on his face, despite the shadow of his hat brim, and the way he held his body, ramrod straight, shoulders squared. It was only after the telephone conversation ended that he relaxed, becoming once more the easygoing cowboy.

She stood at the corner, openly watching as a waiter served him a basket of fish and chips, then sat down at the table to help him eat. The two talked and laughed like old friends. A waitress came out of the café, a tall, young woman with caramel-colored hair worn in short, attractive wisps around her face. She carried a tray of drinks and joined the two men at the table. Lily stood with her fingers coiling into fists, watching another woman flirt shamelessly with her Rollie. Her Rollie. Except he wasn't, of course. And neither should he be.

Lily turned away, intent on going about her business. She wanted a package of specially coated rubber bands for her hair, a new book, a bottle of the cheap oil that gave her nails such a high sheen when buffed. She wanted a candy bar. She wanted to walk about unrecognized, window shopping and observing the bustle around her. This time of freedom was precious to her. Slipping out to the stables was one thing; going off into town on her own was another. It required careful planning and some tricky maneuvering to get out of the castle without at least one bodyguard. She'd borrowed one of the staff's cars today, a tiny, battered subcompact with a tricky third gear, but that wasn't always possible. This day of freedom was a rare treat, and she intended to enjoy it, Rollie Thomas or no Rollie Thomas. So determined, she turned around and walked straight over to his table.

He looked up as she approached and registered an instant of shock. The next moment he was on his feet and sweeping off his hat. "Lily!"

"Rollie, fancy meeting you here. I didn't know you were coming to town."

"It's my regular afternoon off, and Jock insisted I get out from underfoot for a while."

"It's my afternoon, too. I had to get a little shopping done."

She was very aware of the man standing to her left and the woman sitting to her right. She nodded a smile at each, then turned her brightest face on Rollie as he hurried around to pull out a chair for her, saying, "Join us, please."

"Thank you."

He saw her seated and circled around to his own chair, clapping the waiter on the shoulder as he did so. "Let me introduce you. These are my friends, Abby and Walston Shivers."

Lily perked up. A married couple then. As if reading her thoughts, the woman said, "My brother and I own this place together." Lily's smile dimmed. Siblings. Rats.

"How exciting," she murmured as Rollie retook his chair.

"Abby, Wals, this is Lily, uh..."

"Franks," she supplied, completely off the top of her head.

"Lily works at the castle," Rollie smilingly informed the other two.

"Oh, yes, but being a lady's maid is not nearly so interesting as running a restaurant," Lily said quickly. She turned her smile on Wals Shivers and noted absently that he was quite a good-looking man with stylishly short hair very like his sister's and large, sheepish, moss-green eyes. "How did you come to be in the restaurant business, Mr. Shivers?"

"Wals, please," he said, waving away the formal address. "I came by it naturally, as it happens. Our parents are restaurateurs in London."

"Our older brother has a place in Wynborough," Abby put in, "and our sister and brother-in-law run a restaurant in France."

"As the youngest," Wals began.

"And twins," Abby added.

"Everyone wanted to make a place for us."

"But we elected to come here."

"We purchased the place from an elderly couple whose own family was uninterested in maintaining the business," Wals finished.

"And they've made great improvements, according to the locals," Rollie said.

"Can we get you something?" Wals asked. "Abby brews an excellent cup of tea."

"The coffee is otherworldly," Rollie promised, lifting his own cup.

Lily reserved her smile for him. "The coffee sounds wonderful."

For a long moment, no one moved or said a word. Then Lily realized that Wals was glaring at his sister, and Abby finally got up, reluctance coloring her every movement. Lily pretended not to notice while Rollie urged her to taste the fish and chips. Lily nibbled politely, finding both dishes quite tasty. Abby returned posthaste with the coffee, which was, indeed, wonderful.

Talk remained impersonal and light, touching on such topics as the glorious weather, food, horses and a new club opening in town.

"Do you dance, Rollie?" Abby asked. "They'll be having a country-western night, we're told. Perhaps you'll come and go with us?"

"Sounds like fun," Rollie answered. "We'll have to set something up. What do you say, Lily? Interested in a night out on the town?"

She shouldn't. In fact, she couldn't. With great reluctance, she managed to shake her head. "I don't think I can. It's frowned upon, actually, by my, er, superiors."

"Oh, too bad," Abby said, sounding anything but disappointed.

"Wouldn't hurt to ask," Rollie prodded.

"What can they do but refuse you permission?" Wals said.

Lily smiled. Knowing it was hopeless, she nevertheless said, "We'll see."

Rollie grinned and winked, and talk turned to music. Deep in her heart, Lily grieved, knowing she could never pull off a night out on her own. Why had she thought that this deception would work? She was as constrained as ever, and that constraint was opening a clear path to Rollie Thomas's heart for Abby Shivers. Why should that matter to her?

Lily finished her coffee and got up to go, saying, "I have a few more things to pick up. It was a pleasure to meet you, Abby, Wals. Nice seeing you again, Rollie."

"Are you here on your own?" he asked, reaching for his hat.

Her heart leapt. "I am, actually."

"I took the bus in. How about you?"

"I drove."

"I could use a ride back to the castle. Mind if I tag along?"

She tried to ratchet down her smile and failed miserably. "Not at all."

He tossed back his coffee, snatched up a last chip from the basket on the table and took a quick leave of his friends, dropping a hand on Wals's shoulder and a kiss on Abby's cheek.

They walked away from the sidewalk café without a backward glance.

"Where to?" he asked, taking her arm lightly in his hand.

"The sundries shop."

"Lead the way."

They spent an hour in the store, giggling at some of the products and puzzling over others. Some they avoided altogether, as if silently but mutually deeming them too embarrassing for a couple still getting to know each other. When Lily had made her purchases, they strolled through the city streets toward the car lot, stopping at a local park to sit on a bench and watch the toddlers playing under the careful eyes of their mothers and nannies. One little boy who realized that he had an audience put on quite a show, mugging around, winking, blowing kisses and finally pretending that an elephant ride on a spring was a bucking bronco. Rollie laughed aloud at the child's antics, but the boy did not actually approach them.

"You like kids," Lily stated, pleased.

Rollie shot her a surprised glance. "Everyone likes kids."

"Oh, but they don't," she insisted. "In fact, among those who hang about at the castle, anyway, children are nothing more than an irritating necessity, and for some not even that."

"You mean those who hang around the prince and princess?"

She nodded. "All that lot think about are parties and more parties."

"What about the prince and princess themselves?"

"They aren't like that," Lily said positively. "The loss of his wife and child marked Damon deeply, and the princess is always talking about the children she wants to have."

"Sounds as if they need a new class of friends."

"Well, that's the problem, isn't it," Lily said. "When you aren't free to go about the world like normal people, you can hardly meet those outside your immediate sphere."

"I don't see why they shouldn't be free to come and go as they please," he said.

"But you wouldn't, would you, not being part of that whole scene."

He opened his mouth to speak, seemed to think better of it, and lapsed into silence. After a time he asked, "Who is it, exactly, who curtails their freedom so?"

She fluttered her hands, frustrated that she couldn't seem

to make him understand. "The world. All the people waiting to take advantage."

He pushed his hat forward and rubbed a hand across the back of his neck. "I don't see how anyone can take advantage of them if they don't allow it."

She studied him for a moment, slightly confused. "But people are always trying to get something out of them, money usually."

"Short of robbery or kidnapping, Lily, I don't see how they can, unless the Montagues allow it, of course."

"There is that threat, yes."

"But I shouldn't think the threat is any greater for the royals than for any others with wealth, provided they keep a low profile," he said.

She gusted a sigh, quite certain now that she could never make him understand. "That's easier said than done," she told him. "I know. I see Princess Lillian struggling to stay in the background, out of harm's way, but even then the only way she can ever go out is under heavy guard. Even Prince Damon has relative freedom compared to her."

"Perhaps the princess should learn to exert herself a bit more, demand a little respect," Roland muttered.

Lily bit her lip. "You just don't understand. She's been hurt, used. She has to protect herself."

Rollie repositioned his hat and leaned forward, clasping his hands together over his knees. "Seems to me like she's buried herself behind the walls of the castle. I sure haven't laid eyes on her since I've been there. So how can she expect to meet anyone but those who are allowed to come to her? If she really wanted to break out of her royal cage, she could do so, but it would mean developing some backbone and taking a few chances. Sounds to me as if your Princess Lillian just doesn't have what it takes."

Lily frowned down at her own hands clasped tightly in

her lap. So that was it then. She could never tell him who she really was. He simply couldn't understand. No one had ever promised love and wholehearted acceptance to him, only to betray him for cold hard cash. No one had crushed his trust, abused his affections, set out purposefully to bring him under her influence and all in a scheme to get rich quick. Rollie had no reason to mistrust his own judgment, and he wouldn't understand what she had to do to protect herself.

She realized suddenly that she had been hoping for more. For long-term. Perhaps even for permanence. On the basis of a few hours together, she had let herself begin to dream. He was right. She was a fool. She was the one who couldn't be trusted, the reason she must be guarded. She was the reason this *flirtation* with Rollie Thomas could never be anything more than just that.

Chapter Four

He was restless. He liked working with the horses, especially the palomino, which was turning into a rare mount that he'd have liked to breed with the stallion that awaited him back home in Thortonburg, but his investigation had revealed nothing, and he couldn't get his unknown sister out of his mind. Shouldn't he be able to do more, contribute more? None of the information he'd uncovered had revealed the slightest suggestion of his sister's whereabouts. And why was Lily avoiding him?

There. That was the real problem, the real reason he couldn't get out of sight of the mare. Lance Grayson had urged him to stay in place at Roxbury and keep his eyes open while he checked out all the information Roland had given him. He had even praised the kind of data that Roland was able to accumulate, intimating that it was exactly the sort of thing they needed. Roland was doing all that he could here, and it was more than Rafe was able to do. His brother had complained loud and long about that the last time they'd talked on the phone. Roland knew that he would be doing the same thing if he went back to Thortonburg now. No, the reason for this restlessness, this dissatisfaction that kept him watching and waiting, was about five-two and built like every man's dream. And he hadn't laid eyes on her for two days.

Sighing with self-disgust, he pushed away from the mare's stall gate and turned, walking smack into Damon Montague, Prince of Roxbury. Roland quickly ducked his head, lamenting the lack of his hat, which he'd left on the desk in Jock's office. "Sorry."

"My fault," Montague said at the same time.

"Beg your pardon," Roland murmured, turning away.

Damon took a step after him, saying, "Don't I know you?"

Roland stopped, half-turned, lifted a hand to scratch his ear, all the while trying his best to seem relaxed, unaffected. "Of course, Your Highness. I work here. Name's Thomas, Rollie Thomas."

"No, I didn't mean that," Damon said thoughtfully. "You look oddly familiar to me, as if we've met before."

Roland dropped his hand and lifted his chin, knowing perfectly well that the only way out of this was to brazen his way through. "I can't say as how we've actually met, Your Highness, but you're a horseman, so I suppose it's possible we've run across each other before. America, perhaps? Or the markets in Ireland?"

Damon shook his head. "Sorry, no. I must be mistaken."

"Well, it could've been England or Belgium," Rollie suggested disingenuously. "Or even Spain, I suppose, but I was little more than a boy then."

Damon shook his head again. "No, I'm afraid not. I like to ride, but I don't involve myself overmuch with the stock lines. That's Jock's job, and he mostly confers with my sister about it. She's the real horse person around here."

"Odd that," Roland said, and could have bitten his tongue off, but he went on anyway, curiosity getting the better of him. "I don't think I've met Her Highness."

"Well, she's a little shy," Damon said. "She keeps her distance from the male staff, all but Jock."

The male staff.

"I see. Is that a policy I should know about then?"

"No, no, not really," Damon said a little impatiently.

"Because I wouldn't want to overstep," Roland went on quickly.

"I appreciate that," Damon said. Then he grimaced and reluctantly explained. "I suppose we are a bit overprotective. She had an unfortunate experience some years ago, an inappropriate friendship that turned out to be a deliberate extortion attempt."

A friendship that turned out to be a deliberate extortion attempt. Roland suddenly recalled the conversation he'd had with Lily in the park. *She's been hurt, used. She has to protect herself.* It all suddenly, terribly made sense. Some man, likely a servant, had broken the princess's heart by cultivating a relationship with her and then attempting to extort money to cover it up. The poor woman was a prisoner in more ways than one, and he'd openly criticized her to Lily, who was no doubt that woman's dearest friend and confidante, a position Lily would consider a privilege and responsibility. He had offended her, and that was why she had been staying away. He had to apologize. First, however, he had to take his leave of Damon without raising any suspicions.

"That is unfortunate," he said sympathetically. "Jock is nothing if not trustworthy, though. He's a good man."

"Yes, he is."

"Can I assist you in some way, Your Highness? Are you needing a mount saddled?"

Damon pushed a hand through his hair. ''I'm needing a place to hide,'' he confided with a smile. Then he shook his head. ''No. No, thank you, Thomas. Carry on.''

Roland sketched what he sensed was a completely unnecessary bow and got out of there, hoping that ''Rollie'' would forever disappear into the mists of Damon Montague's mind, leaving only a faint impression of ''Thomas'' behind.

Roland waited until he was certain that Prince Damon had left the large stone building that housed the royal stables before approaching Jock, who sat with his back to the office door, pecking on the keyboard of the computer, filling in spaces on a London race form. Roland cleared his throat. Jock jumped, hit a key and cursed as the screen blinked and changed.

''Look what you've made me do!'' he roared, swiveling around in his chair.

Unrepentant, Roland grinned. ''Accidentally put your money on the wrong horse, Jock?''

Scowling, Jock whirled his chair back to face the computer screen and began clicking icons with the mouse pointer. A message blasted onto the screen, proclaiming that the window was closed. Jock whacked a fist on the arm of his chair and turned once more to glare at Roland. ''You cost me my chance to back that newcomer, boyo. You better pray that Spanish Rigger doesn't win this one.''

''He won't,'' Roland replied assuredly.

''And just how could you be knowing that?''

Roland shrugged. ''It's a matter of strategy, Jock. Now if Rigger were mine, I'd want him coming in second or third this race, in the money but not on top.''

''And why would that be?'' Jock scoffed, clearly skeptical.

"Because," Roland explained, "a no-win/money finish in this one will raise the odds for the next."

"Which is the major race," Jock said, suddenly getting it. "The take would skyrocket."

"Provided that Spanish Rigger wins the next one, of course. It's far from foolproof. You can't predict a second-place finish any more than you can predict a win."

Jock made a face. "Damn and blast. Can't even trust the ponies no more. You wouldn't have pulled this stunt yourself, would you, boyo?"

Roland feigned shock "Now when would I have had a chance for that? I just know how these things work." He pointed to the computer screen behind Jock, saying, "They're up."

Jock turned back to the computer a mere second before the horses bolted in jerky real-time broadcast. Two minutes later, a dun named Hardacre streaked across the finish line a neck ahead of Spanish Rigger in second place. "Hmph. Lucky you," Jock grumbled. "I won't have to scar up your pretty face, after all."

It was an empty threat, and Roland knew it, but it brought him to the subject at hand. "Speaking of pretty faces, have you seen Lily lately?"

Jock scratched his chin thoughtfully, then shook his head.

"Could you get a message to her?"

The older man leaned back in his chair, looking far up at Roland. "Now why would I be wanting to do that?"

Roland considered carefully and finally admitted, "I owe her an apology, I think."

"You think?"

Roland grimaced. "I made some disparaging remarks about the princess."

Jock's eyebrows shot into his hairline. "Did you now? And Lily didn't slap your face?"

He flattened his lips. It was worse than he'd thought, then. "She probably wanted to."

"And if I send her this message, what shall I say?" Jock asked carefully.

Roland considered carefully before saying, "That I didn't understand, but now I think I do."

Jock frowned. "Understand what, lad?"

"About the princess, why she keeps to herself, lives like a prisoner in that great house there."

"And what are you understanding about that?" Jock wanted to know.

Roland shrugged. "Only what her brother told me earlier, that she'd been betrayed by a 'friend.'"

Jock snorted. "Friend. He was a jackal, that one." Suddenly, he rocked forward into his chair, proclaiming, "I'll see what I can do." He pointed a knobby finger at Roland. "Now you, boyo, have work to do. That black, the one called Satin, has a swollen fetlock. See what you can do with it, will you?"

Roland saluted cheekily and left the office. He must remember to tell Rafe to get a message to his jockey in London, congratulating him on a well-ridden race.

Lily paused in the night shadows beside the arched, stone entrance to the stables, wondering what in heaven's name she expected to accomplish by coming here again. Nothing good could come of it. How could she possibly trust Rollie? Even if he had not yet discovered her actual identity, everything was bound to change once he did. She had lied to him, and he wouldn't like that—unless he was as opportunistic and unscrupulous as— She shook her head. She couldn't believe that of Rollie, and the fact that she couldn't scared her half to death. How much smarter it would be to walk back the way she'd come and forget Rollie Thomas existed.

She ran a hand over the rough, closely fitted stones of the wall, wondering how many people over the centuries had passed beneath this arch. How many had sought refuge here from one thing or another in their lives? How many lovers, how many fiends, how many lost, uncertain souls had used this same path? After another moment's hesitation, she stepped into the deep black shadow of the arch and eased along it. The warm glow of a lamp beckoned just yards away, but before she reached it, an unexpected voice reached her.

"I thought you'd never come."

She gasped and jerked back against the wall of the archway even as she recognized Rollie. "You frightened me."

"I'm sorry. It wasn't my intention. I was waiting for you."

She rubbed her hands over her arms beneath the heavy cable-knit of her sweater. "I—I couldn't get away until now. Jock said you wanted to talk to me."

"Let's walk down to check on Lady Doubloon," he said, taking her elbow in his big, warm hand. She let him guide her into the wide center aisle of the dimly lit building, listening to the soft whickers and clumps coming from the individual stalls. "You've been angry with me," he began.

She shook her head, surprised. "No, not at all."

"Disappointed in me, then," he went on doggedly. "Don't deny it, just listen for a moment, please. I think we need to clear the air."

"But there's nothing to say."

He stopped, drawing her around to face him. "Won't you even let me try to put things right?" he asked softly. "I've missed you."

If she could have denied the warm infusion of delight his words provided, she would have. As it was, she could only bow her head and hope that he didn't read the naked longing in her eyes. "I've been busy," she murmured.

"Mm-hmm, ever since you tried to explain the princess to me, and I so blithely disparaged her," he said. "I understand better now. I wanted you to know."

She lifted a sharpened gaze. "What is it you understand?"

He turned her and started her down the aisle once more at a slow, easy stroll. "I had a brief conversation with Prince Damon yesterday."

"Oh?"

Rollie nodded. "He was hiding out, from the tempting triplets, I imagine."

Lily giggled, remembering the particularly competitive manner in which the three had tried to corner Damon's attention that day. "Poor Damon."

"Yes, I think he was feeling rather hunted," Rollie commented. "We didn't talk long, but he said enough to help me understand that his sister was betrayed by someone she trusted, perhaps even someone she loved. I understand her behavior a bit better now, and I realize that I judged her too harshly before."

Lily clasped her hands behind her back and carefully thought through both his words and her reply. "She has to protect herself. She would be foolish not to after what she's been through, but her situation really has nothing to do with you and me."

"Doesn't it?" he asked, mimicking her pose. For a long moment nothing else was said. They reached Lady Doubloon's stall and turned to lean against the gate, Lily climbing up onto the bottom rung in order to hook her elbows over the top rail. Doubloon stood facing them and nodded her great, beautiful head at their appearance. Minutes passed amid crooning displays of affection while the mare snuffled every possible hiding place for treats. Lily laughingly fed the horse a chunk of carrot and several sugar cubes. Glancing in his direction, she discovered Rollie watching her, a grin on his face. "I really have missed you," he said. Lily looked away, unable to bear those blazing blue eyes any longer. Rollie cleared his throat. "Were you with the princess when it happened?" he asked lightly.

Lily nodded. "Yes, I was."

"Care to tell me about it?"

Suddenly it seemed important that she do so, and she got down off the gate, turning her back to lean against it. "His name was Spencer. He was older than her, very good-looking and rather worldly."

"Am I right in assuming that he worked here?" Rollie asked, turning so that he partially faced her, only one elbow hooked over the gate.

"Groundskeeper and gardener," she confirmed. "He had a real knack for it. The Thortons have always kept fresh flowers in the public rooms of the castle, but he used to bring armfuls of them every day and present them to the princess as if they were for her alone." Lily smiled to herself, finding it oddly easy to speak about it as if it had happened to someone else. "Naturally, she was flattered. It was such a simple thing to do, very romantic."

"Sounds like a real operator," Rollie murmured.

"Oh, very," she agreed. "He used to say what else did he have to offer her but those flowers? Then one day he answered his own question by adding, 'except my heart.' I'm sure he knew that because of her youth her parents would not approve, so he engineered seemingly innocent private meetings."

"But did they stay 'seemingly innocent?'" Rollie asked doubtfully.

Lily shook her head, too ashamed even to look at him. "No, of course they didn't. Oh, he never took it too far, but she…I think she would have let him."

"She was in love," Rollie said, sighing, and Lily nodded.

"Yes, for the first time. He, of course, vowed undying love, constantly bemoaning the fact that he had nothing to give her except that. When she had assured him sufficiently that his love would be enough for her, he began to hint that a momentous decision was coming. One night he said that they needed every possible argument on their side if he was to approach her father, and he asked her to come to his room." Lily paused to swallow, remembering her own gullibility, what she'd been willing to do that night.

"Naturally she went," Rollie said, rubbing his chin with his hand. "God, I'm surprised Damon didn't kill him."

She smiled bitterly and went on with the story. "He said that if they were already lovers, her father would not object. She was terribly nervous, but she let him undress her, let him seduce her. At the last moment she lost her nerve, but the damage was already done. He had cameras hidden, and he'd asked her repeatedly if she wanted 'it,' making it clear that she was a willing participant."

"Please tell me someone hurt him," Rollie muttered darkly. Lily only sighed.

"No one's ever said exactly what transpired when Spencer approached Prince Charles with that tape," she said, "but no money was paid, and Damon swears that Spencer is not within a thousand miles and won't return. I can't imagine that, wherever he is, he still has such a pretty face. All I know for sure is that when the depth of his betrayal was revealed, the princess ceased to be the same person."

Rollie turned back to face the stall. He bowed his head, obviously thinking. Lily bit her lip, then asked, "You won't repeat any of this, will you?"

He sent her a hooded look. "Do you even have to ask that?"

She glanced away, unable to answer him. He rubbed a hand over his face and turned to put his own back to the stall gate.

"I won't say a word. The princess doesn't really even concern me in this, but I understand that she deserves protection."

Lily turned a puzzled gaze up at him. "Well, if she doesn't concern you, why are we talking about this?"

"Because I want to get back into your good graces," he confessed. "I offended you by failing to understand your defense of your lady. That's what concerns me. I need you to know how much I admire your loyalty to her and that I understand what you were attempting to tell me that day. I was wrong to judge her as I did, but surely you realize that I wasn't criticizing you."

"I didn't think you were," she said honestly. He stared down at her, and she could see that he was trying to understand.

"Then why have you been avoiding me?"

She opened her mouth and closed it again, uncertain what to say to him. How could she explain that his opinion of Princess Lillian was important because she, Lily, was the princess? On the other hand, how could she accept him at face value? What if he knew or suspected the truth? What if he was another Spencer? She shook her head, terribly confused, even by her own feelings.

"Lily," he said, drawing her around to face him fully. "I didn't mean to offend you."

She shook her head helplessly. "I wasn't offended. I've just been busy, truly."

"Then you aren't avoiding me?" he asked softly, curling a finger beneath her chin and turning her face up.

"No," she lied, and was instantly warmed by his smile.

His hand skimmed her cheek briefly. "Will I see you tomorrow?"

She thought of a dozen excuses, then heard herself saying, "Yes."

"I want desperately to kiss you," he whispered. "Do you mind?"

Mind? she thought wildly, lost somewhere in his eyes. She should have minded, and she should have said so, yet her mouth failed to open. He slid his hand beneath her hair at the back of her neck and bent his head to hers. His lips brushed hers and then returned to gently settle, only to break away so that he could nip at her with his teeth and flick his tongue over her lower lip, holding her at the very edge of expectation. By the time he settled into the kiss again, she had curled her fingers into his shirt front. Then he pressed her back against the stall gate and proceeded to set fire to her body. She slid her arms around his neck and willingly gave herself up to the flames. In short order the fire had seared her skin, boiled the blood in her veins, melted her insides and reduced her to a puddle of quivering need. It wasn't at all the thing for a princess, not at all dignified or contained or appropriate—and all the more heady for it.

This was not Lillian Montague, Princess of Roxbury, whom he was kissing. As far as he was concerned, he was holding Lily, lady's maid, in his arms. He couldn't be after anything but the obvious—her. He couldn't be planning to ask for a pay-off from her family later in order to spare her reputation. He couldn't be envisioning a role for himself as royal consort. The very worst he could be planning was an affair with simple, normal Lily. Whatever his purpose, it had to do with Lily herself, not her station in life, and the knowledge acted on Lily like gasoline on a fire.

She went up on tiptoe and pressed herself against him. He made a sound deep in his chest and crushed her against the gate, his tongue simultaneously thrusting into the cavern of her mouth. She tasted possession on his tongue and breathed passion from his lungs. Her head was spinning when the loud, hoarse clearing of a throat alerted them both that they were not alone.

Rollie jerked away and whirled around, shielding her with his body. He muttered a curse then, ending with, "I never could abide a watchdog, Jock." Lily smiled against his back, a hand pressed between his shoulder blades. That had come out with a definitive air of command, as if he were more used to giving than taking orders.

"Is that right?" Jock was saying. "What a pity, that is. Now you just take yourself off so I can speak to the lass."

"I don't think so," Rollie retorted. "Lily doesn't need dressing down. She's—"

"Quite capable of speaking for herself," Lily said smartly, stepping out from behind him.

Rollie relaxed his belligerent stance somewhat, saying, "He has no right to tell us what we can do."

"No, he doesn't," she agreed firmly, "but he has a right to care, and I'm glad to speak to him." She went up on tiptoe and kissed Rollie's cheek. "Go on," she said, smiling. "I'll see you tomorrow."

"You're sure?" he asked protectively, and the sound of concern in his voice set off a little thrill inside her chest.

"Yes, very sure. Thank you. Go now, and let me speak to Jock."

She could tell that he was reluctant, but he finally nodded, dropped a kiss on her forehead and went away, glaring at Jock as he did so. She almost laughed. He had the territorial look about him of the very watchdog he professed to disparage. He looked, too, as though he was fully capable of taking on the world at that moment, if that was what she required. She watched him saunter down the aisle toward the staircase at its far end. His would be one of several rooms overhead. She imagined that his head almost scraped the low, beamed ceiling and his lithe frame hung off the end of his bed. When he had disappeared into the stairwell, she turned a glare of her own on Jock.

"So you think I need a watchdog, do you, Jock?"

The old man opened his mouth, closed it again, and coughed into his fist before saying, "I promised your mum—"

"You've made Mother any number of promises over the years," she reminded him shortly, "most of which you ignore as it suits you." She folded her arms. "Just which one of us is it that you don't trust, Jock? Me or Rollie?"

Jock pursed his lips, rocked back on his heels and admitted, "As to that, I trust you both, lass, I do."

Lily had half expected him to tell her that it was Rollie of whom he was unsure, and only when he did not did she realize how great her relief was to hear otherwise. She leaned back against the stall gate. "So you don't think Rollie's out to use me?"

Jock scratched his chin. "No, I don't. Mind you, I'm not quite sure what he is after, but I'd stake me life that he means you no harm."

"But you think he's after something here?" she asked with some alarm.

Jock cocked his head. "I didn't say that now. It's only that he's an uncommon man, our Rollie. Or haven't you noticed that?"

"I've noticed," she said softly.

"Well, then, I canna be blamed for wondering what a man such as that one is doing mucking stalls, even if it is for one of the finest stables in the world, now can I?"

"Perhaps he came to learn at the feet of the great Jock Browning," she suggested teasingly.

Jock snorted. "That one has never sat at another's feet, lass. You can mark my words on that. Oh, he's obedient and a good worker, very thorough, but he's biding his time here, and that's what worries me."

Lily considered that before asking, "And what am I doing, Jock, if not biding my time, and for what, for whom?"

"Those are questions only you can answer, my sweet," Jock told her gently, "decisions only you can make."

"Then let *me* make them, Jock," she said, and he grinned.

"Aye. So I will then, and proud I am of you for insisting on it."

She shook her head. "You absolutely delight in confounding me, don't you?"

"Noooo," he insisted. "I love you, lass, that's all."

She laughed. "And how do you feel about Rollie Thomas?"

"Well, I wouldn't be kissing him on the mouth," Jock teased, "but I like the man, even if he does puzzle me a bit. Just go easy there, lass. Be very sure what it is you want from him and that he's willing to give it."

"Easier said than done, Jock," Lily whispered. "I'm almost afraid to find out what I do want."

"And now who's not trusting herself?" Jock demanded. "You've already dealt with the villain, lass. Can you not trust yourself to recognize him when you see him again?"

Lily took a deep breath and answered the only way she knew how. "I hope so, Jock. I hope so."

"I know so," Jock said. "Truth be told, I'm glad to see you letting down your guard at long last. Just don't settle for less than you're due."

Lily smiled. "You speak as though you consider Rollie a fitting match for a princess," she quipped.

He shook his head. "No such thing, not for my princess. But what man could be?" He sighed. "I fear we have to make do with what the world offers."

She laughed. "So we do, Jock. So we do."

Chapter Five

"Can't hurt to ask," Roland said encouragingly, leaning back against the step above him. He and Lily were sitting on the stairs that led up to his room, discussing their plans for their mutual midweek day off, speaking quietly in order to evade the sharp ears of Jock the watchdog. Since neither had to report to work the next day, it seemed as good a time as any to pay a visit to the club in town. "Abby says the music is quite good," he went on, "and Wals assures me that the crowd is well-behaved."

"I'll ask," Lily said, "but don't count on it."

"We won't call attention to ourselves," Roland promised gently. "I only want to dance with you." It was a lie; he wanted much more than a dance with the delectable Lily—more than information, even.

"It's not quite that simple," Lily answered. "When one is associated personally with the royal family, there are standards, high standards, to be kept."

He wanted to go on arguing. He wanted to walk into that club with Lily on his arm. He had only agreed to the outing because he had anticipated dancing with her, but there were limits beyond which he could not press. He was well aware of the need for trustworthy servants by those in the position of the Montagues. His own father was Draconian when it came to the standards imposed upon Thorton family servants. The royal fishbowl did not allow for public missteps even by the hired help, especially if they were in positions that put them in close proximity to the family. Roland understood the reasons for the rules quite well, he had just never before seen the situation from this perspective. He would be more understanding in the future, he decided, with his own personal staff. Meanwhile, he was developing a new sensitivity to Lily's position. His own job might not be jeopardized by a night on the town, but hers certainly could be, not that he would allow her to get into trouble. He shook his head. For the first time, what he would allow did not count for much.

"If you don't go, I won't go," he said decisively. "It's not that important."

Lily swept a glance over his face and asked, "What about Abby?"

"What about her?"

Lily hitched a shoulder. "I think she'll be disappointed."

"That's her problem."

Sitting on the step above him, she twisted to wedge her back against the wall, her knees drawn up. "How long have you known the Shivers?" she asked idly.

"Not long. Met them the first day I was here. The bus stops in front of their café, you know. Why do you ask?"

She looked down at her hands in the half-light. "I just wondered how well you know Abby."

Much to his satisfaction, he recognized the hint of jealousy in her carefully modulated tone. "We've shared meals together a few times," he said softly, "the three of us. But

I've never been alone with her, and I've never wanted to be."

Lily lifted her gaze to his, a smile in her eyes. "She likes you."

"I like her, too," he said. Then, even knowing that he shouldn't, he leaned close and whispered, "But she's not the one who's been keeping me up nights lately."

Lily's smile touched her mouth this time. "Are you saying I have?"

He lifted an eyebrow. They were on dangerous ground. He should stop himself from flirting with her. He should, but he didn't. "Oh, my lovely, yes."

"How would I be keeping you up nights?" she asked coyly.

He could have told her; instead, he chose to demonstrate. Sliding a hand beneath the luxurious fall of her hair, he clamped it around the nape of her neck to pull her mouth down to his. She closed her eyes, and her fingertips danced along his jaw line. Her mouth against his was a very sweet thing. It filled him with a heady sense of well-being and a raging desire for more. Abandoning any hope of good sense, he dropped his hand and slid an arm around her waist, pulling her down to his level. He stretched out his long frame, leaning back on one elbow while keeping the other arm wrapped around her waist. She sprawled against him, one hip wedged on the step next to his. He lay back fully, curling both arms around her and pulling her partially across him. All the while, her mouth clung to his greedily, employing lips and tongue and teeth in an apparent effort to drive him mad. It was working. Oh, how well it was working.

The clop of hooves on cobblestones and the call of voices, Jock's among them, brought Roland back from the edge of delicious insanity. Groaning with regret, he broke the kiss. "Company," he murmured.

With a little gasp, Lily rolled away to sit on the narrow step next to him, smoothing her long, golden hair with her hands. Roland cleared his throat and willed his body to quiescence. He wouldn't blame her if she slapped his face. Instead, stars danced in her eyes. Lord, help him. He was insane to play such games with her. He'd have to do better. She deserved it.

"I should go help them," he said after a moment. "They've brought a fresh string in from the paddock, and some of the horses are always reluctant to return to the stalls."

Lily nodded, her gaze sparkling with want. "Go on," she said lightly. "I'll just sit here for another minute."

He eased to his feet three steps farther down, then turned and leaned forward, trapping her between his arms, hands braced against the step upon which she sat. So much for doing better. "Will I see you later?"

She answered simply, without the least guile or pretense. "Yes."

Smiling, he kissed her quickly and turned to hurry out into the stable proper. Only later, as he was leading a balky chestnut into a center stall, did he realize that he'd forgotten to quiz her, as Lance had recently suggested, about the Wynborough shipping contract and what the Montagues might be willing to do to ensure that they won it. Lately that forgetfulness was becoming a habit. He reminded himself sternly that his sister's safety depended on him and the rest of the family. Whether or not he ever got to dance with Lily was very much beside the point—even if it did feel, somehow, like everything.

It just couldn't be done. Lily knew that, and yet she plotted and planned. She had managed to find moments of freedom away from their guests during the days without too much difficulty, but opting out of an evening of entertainment was problematic for any hostess and especially so for Lily, since her mother had been called away for a few days by duties elsewhere. Frankly, Lily just wished the whole lot of them would go away, as some of the better mannered had done, but she knew that wasn't likely to happen. These so-called "house parties" sometimes lasted a month or more, and many of their friends led lives of such complete frivolity that it never occurred to them that others might have something productive to do. They literally had nowhere to go and nothing to do until another party was organized elsewhere. Lily wished her mother had not issued the invitation that had brought them all here this time, but she doubted that she wished it any more than Damon did. Poor, pursued Damon.

After much musing and many rejected schemes, Lily decided that her only hope was to approach her brother. He could certainly understand her need to get away from the castle for an evening. Unfortunately, he understood so well that he first proposed accompanying her wherever she wished to go. Since that would be disastrous to her little masquerade, she quickly declined. Damon, however, knew her too well. He insisted on knowing what it was that could pull his normally semi-reclusive sister away from the castle at night, and he continued insisting until she told him about the club. His next suggestion was even more potentially disastrous than the first. The whole lot of them would go, he exclaimed. Horrified, she immediately nixed that idea, saying that on second thought the place was bound to be overrun with locals. It would be better—safer—just to put on some good music and stage their own dance.

Thankfully, Damon agreed with her. Irritatingly, he insisted on playing the protective big brother to the hilt and demanded to know how she'd come to hear of the new club in town. In desperation Lily told a half-lie. She had "overheard" one of the stable hands talking about it. Seemingly unconvinced, Damon wanted the man's name. She probably shouldn't have mentioned Rollie, but at the time she couldn't for the life of her think of anyone else. As soon as she said it, she saw the light of recognition in Damon's intelligent eyes.

"It's Thomas, isn't it? Rollie Thomas?"

She didn't want to lie to him by saying that she didn't know for sure, so she simply repeated his question back to him. "Is it?"

Damon studied her speculatively, murmuring, "He's a handsome devil, that Thomas."

Lily retreated into sheer prevarication. "Do you think so? I hadn't noticed. Frankly, I'm surprised you did."

"It's hard to miss," Damon said quietly.

She shrugged. "If you say so." Making a valiant attempt to change the subject, she wondered aloud, "What should I wear tonight? Something funky or that floaty little tea dress Mother picked up in Wynborough?"

"You don't have anything *funky*," Damon reminded her dryly.

She made a face. "Okay, the tea dress then."

Smoothly, she turned the conversation to what kind of music they had available on CD and did her level best not to let her disappointment show through. She had known all along that it just wasn't possible, but she had so wanted to dance on Rollie's arm.

They were having a party up at the house. Occasionally someone opened an outside door somewhere, and Roland caught the sound of music on the night air. He stared at the lighted windows and wondered where Lily was and what she was doing. He wondered about himself, too, why he couldn't look away from those lighted windows and strained to hear the errant notes of unrecognizable music instead of going up to his room and losing himself in a good book or joining Jock in his private quarters out back to watch television. The other stable hands had families to go home to, with the exception of one young man who spent nearly all of his free time in town with his girlfriend, often staying through the night. So Roland was usually alone in the evenings. Tonight, he felt very much alone, standing there in the archway, leaning against the cold stone wall, and he needn't be. Jock would welcome his company. The Shivers had requested it. Still, he stood and stared and wondered why he did so.

He didn't realize that he was waiting until he saw her—or, rather, the pale, billowing skirts of her dress as she flitted across the cobblestone yard. He didn't doubt that it was her. Some part of him recognized Lily even before the moonlight caught her golden head and gilded it platinum. Some interesting things happened within his body as she drew near. It was as if a strange burst of energy heightened his senses. The air around him grew sweeter, cleaner, crisper and at the same time heavy with the redolence of the stables. He felt his clothing—actually felt it—against his skin, along with the pulsing of his blood at the base of his throat, in his chest and in his groin. Suddenly the night was filled with the subtle sounds of animals, people, things, all moving, shifting, breathing. The night itself was indolence, and it took all his energy to feel everything that he was feeling. He marveled that she could run so lightly toward him, while he could do no more than stand there with his blood surging and his heart climbing into his throat.

She laughed when she saw him, and such joy seized him

that it was frightening in its intensity. He stepped forward and offered her his hand. She clasped it trustingly, turning him on his heel and pulling him along as she ran into and through the archway. Once in the light, she stopped and whirled to face him, laughing again.

"I didn't think I'd ever get away," she gasped.

Almost without thinking, he asked, "Away from what?"

"The party."

It didn't strike him as particularly odd until he saw the look of wary dismay that suddenly drained the laughter from her face. He stepped back slightly and fully took in her appearance. Her long golden hair had been parted in the middle and rolled up on the sides, the back left to hang down between her shoulder blades, tiny wisps floating about her face. She was wearing makeup, the first he'd ever seen on her face, a soft, moss-green eye shadow, black mascara, bright-red lipstick that made him want desperately to slant his mouth across hers and take everything she had to give—which was considerable, if the promise of that dress held true. Little more than lace and whispers, it floated in pale sea-green layers about her slender body from tiny straps at the shoulders, the skirt flaring just above the knees to flutter about her calves. A pair of silver high-heeled sandals did marvelous things for legs already slender and shapely. She was gloriously breathtaking and definitely outfitted for a party. Did servants have parties on the premises? he wondered.

"They invited me to the party in consolation," she explained breathlessly, "for not being allowed to go to the club."

He blinked at that. "The prince and princess invited you to their party?" he asked dumbly.

"Mm-hmm." She whirled away from him and sauntered down the center aisle, her heels clacking and scraping on the uneven cobblestones. The sway of her hips created a stir in his groin. When she pirouetted on one toe, throwing out her arms and letting her head fall back to expose the long, slender length of her neck, the movement thrust her breasts against the lace and its filmy lining, and his mouth literally watered. She stopped and held out a hand to him. "Dance with me!"

He chuckled, even as he clasped her fingertips with his and pulled her to him. "We don't have any music."

"Don't we?" she asked, floating into his arms.

"A waltz," he said because the count alone could lead them.

She smiled, and he began dancing her up and down the corridor. She closed her eyes and let him sweep her along to a silent song, turning, turning, turning. He laughed, wondering why on earth he'd wanted to take her to that loud, crowded club when he could have had her here like this all along. At last she'd had her fill. Breathless, she sagged against his chest.

"You dance well."

"So do you," he replied softly.

She smiled up into his face. "I don't usually. It's different, dancing with you. Everything's different with you. Why is that, do you think?"

"I have no idea. I know this, though. It's dangerous for us to be alone together. Lately I can't seem to think of anything but making love to you."

If she was shocked in any way, she didn't show it. "You are always so honest," she said, and he inwardly winced.

"It's better to be honest about these things," he said softly. "And I honestly don't think we're ready for making love. Do you?"

For one heart-stopping moment, he thought she was going to say yes, prayed she'd say yes, but then the longing in her eyes changed to resignation, and she shook her head. "Not yet."

Not yet. He took a deep breath and took her hand in his, saying, "Tell me about the party."

"What do you want to know?"

"Everything," he murmured distractedly, wondering where he could take her so they could talk. He started toward the stairs. No, not the stairs. They led up to his room, and even if he didn't succumb to temptation and take her all the way up, he couldn't forget what had happened in the stairwell earlier. He turned toward Jock's office. No, not the office. He could too well imagine the use to which they could put the couch there, or the desk, or the chair. Good grief, was no place safe from his imaginings? The tack room. What lasciviousness could be performed on a wooden sawhorse? "This way."

He gave her no room or time for argument, pulling her along. When she saw what he had in mind, she strolled along freely at his side, her hand clasped in his. Reaching inside the open door, he switched on the overhead light. Saddle horses lined the walls, every manner of adjunct equipment hanging above them from pegs in neat precision. He pulled two of the freestanding saddle horses into the center of the room, then lifted her up to sit sideways on one of the saddles. The other he threw his long leg over and mounted so that he sat facing her, his elbow braced on the saddle horn.

She smiled and looked down at her hands nervously. "I want to, you know."

He didn't have any trouble figuring out that she was talking about sex. "I'm glad to hear it, but it's a big decision, and a girl like you deserves to have these things done right." That was the truth. Lily wasn't the sort of young lady for casual affairs. She deserved a man who would be with her and treasure her from now on, and he couldn't be that man. For one thing, his parents weren't likely to welcome a commoner into the royal family, sticklers that they were. For another, he'd already determined that marriage wasn't for him. Add to that the fact that he'd lied to her about his identity, and he was left with a really unworkable situation.

"I never have before," she said softly, "made love with anyone, I mean."

"I know." He didn't know how he knew, but he did. "Now, maybe you'd better tell me about that party."

She shrugged. "Not much to tell. They were dancing and drinking and playing their music loud, talking, making jokes."

"Did you enjoy yourself?"

She hunched a shoulder. "I just don't seem to have much in common with them, you know."

He did know. Unfortunately that fact was just another of the many secrets he was guarding. He changed the subject. "What kind of music do you like?"

She spread her hands. "Oh, some of everything, I suppose, but really, when you come right down to it, it's hard to improve on the classics in my opinion."

He grinned at her. "My sentiments exactly."

"Really? I thought you'd prefer country-western."

Oops. "Well, I like it, of course. It's great fun to dance to."

"Yes, I've always thought it would be," she said excitedly. "Perhaps you'll teach me sometime?"

"Sure."

"Excellent! I'll bring a portable player down some evening soon, shall I?"

"Why not?" he agreed. If they were dancing, they couldn't be doing anything else, after all, and he'd still be able to question her, which brought him, reluctantly, to the need to do so now. He'd thought about his approach and planned it carefully, so that he didn't have to pause long to come up with the right lead-in. "It must be grand not to have anything more important to do than throw parties. I wonder if the prince and princess know how lucky they are."

"Oh, but they aren't like that," Lily protested. "If it were up to them, they wouldn't be having this house party."

"Then why go on with it?" Roland asked, truly puzzled.

"It's their mother, you see. She wants them both married and settled, especially the prince, and so she keeps arranging these things and obliging them to play the parts of host and hostess. The problem is that the sort who usually answer those kinds of invitations simply do not interest the prince and princess precisely because *they* choose not to party their lives away."

One thing Roland knew too well was the difficulty of dealing with an overbearing parent. He felt a deep kinship with the prince and princess of Roxbury at that moment, and wouldn't his Montague-hating father be appalled by that! All the more reason to acquit himself ably in this mission. He scratched an ear, pretending perplexity. "It seems to me that if the prince and princess had something important to do with themselves, their mother wouldn't be able to impose on them like this."

Lily rolled her eyes. "That's because you have never had to deal with their parent. Let me tell you, Charles is easier to defy."

"Is that so? Still, it doesn't excuse them from leading frivolous lives."

"But that's the point. They don't lead frivolous lives," Lily argued. "The princess is heavily involved in cultural and charitable matters, while the prince is an integral part of the government. Many of the ministers report to him, and he pretty much oversees the family finances, as well. There are several businesses."

"Hmm." Roland fingered his chin thoughtfully, elation pouring through him at the opening she had given him, then he said as casually as he could manage, "You know, I did hear something about a big shipping contract not too long ago."

"Oh, that," she said with an airy wave of her hand. "That's more symbolic than anything else."

"Symbolic?"

"It's an old rivalry," she explained. "No one pays attention to it anymore but Prince Charles." She shrugged and went on easily. "Damon says that King Phillip is scrupulously fair and masterfully diplomatic. Damon expects the contract will be rotated year by year between Thortonburg and Roxbury from now on as a matter of policy."

"But didn't the Thortonburg heir just marry one of the Wynborough princesses?" Roland asked, feigning uncertainty.

Lily nodded. "Yes, which is why we, er, Roxbury, was awarded this year's contract. King Phillip didn't want to be seen playing favorites by awarding the contract to his new in-laws. At least, that's what Damon says and has been saying all along."

Now the questioning became tricky. He could only hope that his interest in the matter did not arouse her suspicion. "What about Prince Charles?" he asked lightly. "Did he share his son's expectations on the contract?"

"He did not," Lily stated emphatically, "but since Damon took over the shipping concern last year, Charles has no say in how it's managed."

"I imagine that Damon's position has been immeasurably strengthened since he was proven right,'' Roland muttered as much to himself as to her.

''Not really,'' Lily said. ''Damon's quite capable of standing firm against unwanted involvement.''

''On his father's part,'' Roland said with a grin.

Lily laughed. ''True. His mother is another matter. Fortunately she's not interested in government or finances.''

Roland nodded, thankful his lovely Lily would never know what a fount of information she was to him. ''You've wrecked all my preconceived notions about royalty,'' he teased. ''No wonder you are so devoted to the Montagues and your position here.''

''My position here?'' she echoed uncertainly, but then she blinked and waved a hand dismissively. ''That means nothing.''

He gaped. ''I beg your pardon?''

''Oh, I mean, I need the job, of course,'' she quickly said, ''but it's just until something better comes along, something more.''

He could only scratch his head at that. ''I'm sorry, Lily, but I don't see that happening. If it's a better job you want, you have to go out and get it, and as far as service goes, is there a better position than with a royal family?''

She smiled almost sadly. ''You don't understand. It's not a job I'm waiting for, it's a life, a life of my own, a family of my own, a husband. I guess what I'm waiting for is love.''

He felt as if she'd kicked him in the chest. ''Love, ah, do you think it's really possible, the kind of love the romantics tout?''

''You don't?'' she countered warily.

He found himself wanting to lie to her, to offer her hope where none existed, at least in his mind. He didn't. ''I doubt it. I've certainly not seen it, anyway.''

"What about your parents?" she asked, clearly appalled.

He thought of his parents, of the recent changes he had sensed. Was there more to their marriage than he had assumed? Or were these little displays of affection and emotion merely the product of this crisis, this kidnapping? He shook his head. Years of established behavior would not change permanently. After the crisis was past, the "status quo" would undoubtedly return.

"Their marriage is one of convenience," he said. "Even now, after all these years, it seems cold and one-sided to me. I mean, I think my mother loves my father. She would have to, frankly, but he..." Roland let the thought drift away.

"That's the saddest thing I've ever heard," Lily said gently. "What about your grandparents?"

Roland rolled his eyes. "They were barely civil to each other. Believe me, that was no love match. My brother, now, that may be another story, but time will only tell, I suppose."

They chatted about his brother whom Roland carefully didn't name for a time. Roland told her only that he was in construction and recently married, much to their parents' delight.

"Surely they wouldn't be so pleased for him if their own marriage wasn't happy," Lily said thoughtfully.

Roland shrugged. "I think it's more a matter of grandchildren, frankly. There's one on the way, as a matter of fact. Oh, don't get me wrong, I'm sure my brother's happiness matters to them—well, to Mother, anyway. As far as Father is concerned, though, having his own way is always paramount. It's not without its conveniences for me, though, my brother's marriage. I mean, since he is the, er, favorite, it rather lets me off the hook, so to speak."

"In other words, they aren't expecting you to marry," Lily surmised.

"I don't see why they would," Roland replied. "I doubt they've even considered whether or not I shall marry one day. In their eyes, I've never measured up to my older brother and I never will, so why bother about my future?"

"I can't believe they're so indifferent," Lily said softly.

Roland shrugged. "Perhaps they aren't. Perhaps the failings are all mine."

"Or perhaps they're an excuse for you to do just as you want," Lily mused softly. "You don't believe in love, and no one expects you to marry, so you've simply decided not to. Is that about right?"

Why did he hesitate to agree? She was exactly right. The logic of it was patently obvious, and yet something held him back. He pushed the feeling away, cleared his throat and said what he had to. "Yes."

She looked away briefly, but then she turned a bright countenance on him and inquired happily, "So what do you mean to do with the rest of your life, Rollie Thomas? I won't believe you're destined to remain in this stable forever."

Roland smiled. "I'm going to have a ranch," he said, no trace of doubt in his voice, "and raise the finest horses in this wide world."

Lily clapped her hands with such delight that he launched into a detailed description of the place he would build and the horses he would breed. Anxious to turn the subject from marriage and family and encouraged by her obvious enthusiasm, he talked a long while, his own excitement growing as he spoke the words aloud, painted pictures and dreams with them, and held her in thrall as he did so. It occurred to him, once or twice, that he had never spoken to anyone else this way, never revealed so much of his hopes and plans, but then she would ask another question, and he would be off again, oblivious of everything but the need to tell this woman what was in his heart of hearts. The funny thing was, he had such a good time doing it. When, he had to wonder, had such a simple thing as talking been such a pleasure for him? Why couldn't he help thinking that it must have something to do with the person who was listening?

And why did that thought send shivers up his spine? A man who didn't believe in love had no reason to shiver. Or was it that a man who didn't believe in love had no reason, period? Suddenly he was afraid to know. Suddenly, he was very much afraid—for both of them.

Chapter Six

He was amazing. Lily listened to the words pour out of Rollie, and in her mind's eye she saw it all taking shape, the house and barns of white stone, their green roofs making them seem a natural part of the landscape, the corral fences stitching together the gently rolling hills and buildings into a lush, homey mosaic where horses would run with their tails in the air and their manes flowing free. All his picture lacked was a family with whom to share it, a wife and children to take pride in his accomplishments, and work and play at his side.

Her heart ached to think that he might go through his life alone. If only she could convince him that love did exist, the kind of love that could last a lifetime and endure against all difficulties. She knew it was true, because if that kind of love did not exist, life was not worth living. Funny how she had never quite thought of it that way before, though. After Spencer, she had somehow started to think of love as a dangerous, risky thing to be avoided. Only lately had she come to realize that she was waiting for someone to make the danger and risk acceptable. Unfortunately, the first man who might conceivably have done that for her was himself closed to the very idea. So she listened to him spill his dreams and ached to share them in more than just the hearing.

When he had seemingly wound down somewhat, she couldn't help prodding him to go on talking until, finally, he was all talked out. He balanced his crossed forearms on the saddle horn and smiled at her, happiness sparkling in his blue eyes. "I can't believe I've told you all this."

"Oh, but it's wonderful!" she exclaimed.

"Do you really think so?"

"It's going to be a great success, I just know it. Jock says you have the finest hand with a horse he's ever seen, and that just reinforces my own opinion. Really, I can't think of anyone better suited for a horse ranch. You'll do wonderfully, Rollie. I know you will."

"Thank you," he said. "That means a lot to me."

"You're welcome."

"If you don't stop me, I'm going to kiss you now," he whispered, leaning closer.

"I won't stop you," she said breathlessly, knowing perfectly well that she should. Like metal shavings drawn by a magnet, they came together, mouth to mouth.

At first, that was all it was, a simple kiss, the touching of lips and nothing more. Then she lifted a hand, tentatively, to skim his shoulder, and the next thing she knew, he was throwing his long leg over the saddle to stand and pull her to him. She went eagerly, sliding her arms around his waist as he bent her head back with the force of his mouth on hers. He clasped her tight, his hands roaming over her back, fitting her to him.

When his fingertips brushed the strap of her dress off her shoulder, she let it fall, shrugging slightly. When his hand slipped around to lightly cup the side of her breast, she knew what he wanted without having to be told. Her heart was pounding so hard that she felt sure he could feel it, but she slipped her arm free of the strap and waited for him to understand. The fabric sagged over the hand at her breast, and suddenly he pulled his mouth from hers and stepped back. Slowly, with agonizing care, he took his hand away, and the soft fabric slid away from her bare breast. For a moment he seemed unable to do anything except stare, but then he lifted his hand once more, and his fingertips skimmed her flesh. She closed her eyes, savoring the electric hot sensation.

"You are perfection," he said huskily, and then his hand covered her breast, squeezing gently.

She thought her knees would buckle. Her peaked nipple pushed against the curve of his palm.

"Sweet heaven," he said, weighing the globe of flesh in his hand. "I should stop now." He squeezed gently again, and his thumb and forefinger moved to lightly pinch her nipple.

She let her head fall back and stiffened her spine, knees locked.

"Tell me to stop," he demanded raspily.

She lifted her head and opened her eyes. The lids were heavy. In fact, a languorous heaviness seemed to have invaded her whole body. Her breast literally seemed to enlarge in his hand. She had never felt anything like this before. Something told her this moment was precious, one of the most precious of her life. "Not yet," she said, amazed that her voice sounded sure and steady. "Don't stop. Not yet."

"Lily," he whispered, almost scolding her as he stepped back, dropping his hand. Suddenly she knew that if she didn't do something, and quickly, it would all be over. And somehow, she knew exactly what to do.

Very deliberately, she reached up and slipped the remaining strap from her other shoulder. The delicate layers of lawn and lace fluttered to the floor, puddling gracefully about her feet, leaving her standing in nothing more than heels, stockings, garter belt and panties.

Rollie stepped back and clapped a hand over his heart, his jaw dropping as his gaze swept her up and down. "Sweet heaven!" He sounded as if he were choking, and for an instant Lily felt the insane urge to giggle, but then he stepped forward once more and hooked an arm around her waist, yanking her hard against him. Her bare flesh felt silky and yielding against his lean, tough body. His jeans and shirt were rough and cool, but she knew that heat lay beneath, melting, searing heat. She lifted a hand to his chest, wanting that heat desperately. "Do you even know what you're doing?" he said between gritted teeth.

"No," she admitted. "I only know that I want it."

"Aw, Lily," he whispered in that scolding tone again, but then his mouth was on hers, his hand cupping the back of her head as his arm tightened about her waist.

It was the next thing to brutal and oddly akin to tender, the way he delved into her with his mouth. He held nothing back—tongue, teeth, lips. His hands splayed against the back of her head and across her buttocks, making her feel every nuance of his kiss, every ridge and valley of his body pressed to hers. She dug her fingertips into the tops of his shoulders and pushed up onto her tiptoes, rubbing against him. He groaned, and both arms came around her, crushing her. She slid her arms around his neck, drawing tighter still, closer but not close enough, even though she could feel her breasts flatten and swell against his chest. Inside she had turned to syrup, hot and sweet and thick like heated molasses, and nothing had ever felt so right to her, so much like herself, so completely her own.

For a long time he held her, kissing her mouth and her face and her neck, the tops of her shoulders, nipping at her with his teeth, touching the tip of his tongue to her skin. He stroked her pliant body with trembling hands, making her know how much he wanted her, showing her the strength and length of his own desire, while she fought to make him understand that she was willing to give him anything, everything. She told him with every nuance, every tiny gasp and hitch in her breath, every curl of her fingertips against his flesh, every subtle gyration of her body, every answering maneuver of her mouth that she was willing, so willing, to give her all. She knew that he heard, felt, sensed her every message, but she knew, too, that as willing as she was, he was not. And it was that fact which broke her heart.

He wanted to. Oh, how he wanted to lift her legs about his waist, sweep away the last barrier and take her there against the wall or the door or, heaven forbid, even the floor. He wanted desperately to bury himself inside her hot core, to lose himself and his scruples in her willing body, to forget the lies he'd told and the truth he'd learned—that Lily deserved better than he could give her. For a time he hoped that he could make himself forget, but the longer he held her, the stronger his desire grew, and the more he knew that he could not indulge himself at her expense. However willing she was at the moment, Lily could not give her body without also giving her heart, and that was a gift he could not take away with him—not and live with himself for the rest of his life.

He knew what he had to do, but he did it only with great difficulty, gently, bit by bit, breaking the kiss and loosening his embrace, until finally he could set her aside, step back and stiffen his resolve with a deep breath. Goodness, but she was beautiful, all pale-gold and cream, her breasts seemingly too full and heavy for her delicate shoulders and slender torso, the impossibly narrow circumference of her waist, the luscious swell of hips plumped to roundness atop long, slim legs and dainty feet to match her long, slim arms and dainty hands. And atop it all, the face of an angel haloed in the spun gold of hair that spilled about her face and shoulders. She was beautiful, and she wanted him as she had wanted no other man, and he had to let her go.

Averting his gaze, determined not to fail in this, he stepped around her, stooped and picked up the dress. Handling it delicately, he held it by the straps hooked over his fingers and brushed away invisible specks of dust with a clumsy hand. Rising to his feet, he held up the dress and looked at it, surprised that he could feel such affection for so inanimate an object. Then he turned and carried the dress to where she stood with her arms crossed over her chest. He smiled, finding that belated bit of modesty endearing.

Deliberately, trying hard not to look at what he was so gallantly giving up, he gathered up the dress and settled it over her head. Slowly, jerkily, she unfolded her arms and slipped them through the straps. The dress slid effortlessly, lovingly into place. *Oh, yes,* he thought, skimming its lacy surface with his hands, a dear, perfect little garment for *a dear, perfect woman.* He closed his eyes and said, "I want you to go back to the house now."

When he looked again, she was staring at him with pleading eyes, and he knew what she wanted, but he couldn't do it. Loving her would be the ruin of her; loving her would be unfair, unkind, but anything less than loving her was unthinkable.

"Go back to the castle," he said roughly. "Go back to the party."

She lifted the fingertips of one hand to her mouth. It had been red with lipstick before; now it was red with the violent thoroughness of his kiss. Would anyone notice? Of course, they would. He would. She stepped toward the door, dragging her toe across the floor reluctantly, and her hand fluttered away from her mouth. She turned then, as if she would say something, and he saw the confusion in her eyes.

"It isn't that I don't want you," he said brokenly, haltingly. "It's that you deserve more—better—than I can offer."

She lifted her chin, looking very regal and commanding in that moment. He wondered if the princess knew how little she had on her lady's maid. A name was not all those two shared.

"That's too bad," his Lily told him smoothly, "because I'm afraid I've become used to getting what I want." With that, she turned and strode purposefully from the room, arms swinging at her sides.

"So am I, lovely Lily," he told her softly. "So am I." He didn't bother to point out, even to himself, that neither of them had managed very well so far.

She was going to have to seduce Rollie Thomas. It was the only solution to their dilemma. Somehow she had to overcome his lovely scruples, slay his doubts and put to rest his fears, and the only way to do it was to get herself into his bed, to bind him to her so completely with the force of their shared desire that he could not break away, would not want to break away. And she had to do it before he found out who she really was.

Now if only she knew how to go about it.

She'd all but stripped herself naked and climbed up on a silver platter, and he'd done nothing more than sample the fare, replace the cover and send her away. Somehow she had to whet his appetite, make him drool and forget all the reasons why he shouldn't indulge. She had to flirt, suggest, hint, entice. But first she had to pray because she hadn't the least idea what she was doing.

She didn't expect those prayers to be answered, frankly. Surely what she planned was sinful. And yet, somehow, it was also right. She belonged with Rollie Thomas, and he belonged with her. She knew it deep within her bones and trusted that knowledge with her whole heart.

The logical place to begin seemed to be her closet. She pulled out every staid, formal, proper item in her substantial collection of clothing and relegated the whole lot to the darkest recesses of her personal storage suite. Then she began assessing each remaining piece for potential appeal. It was a massive undertaking, requiring the majority of three days and twice as many maids. When it was done, she had completely remade her daily wardrobe, which now consisted mostly of pieces deemed too small or too revealing or too "common" before.

The next step was to employ the "wisdom" of her more practiced house guests—the female variety, anyway. To that end, she organized one of those chatty, gossipy, giggly girl things that she usually avoided so assiduously, a nominal "tea" in her private suite. It didn't take much to move the conversation to clothes and then men and then clothes and men. Before long they were bouncing on the bed and playing dress-up like children. It was Lady Margaret Dunlevy—known as Mags to her near and dear—who proved herself fashion consultant to the romantically challenged. Before the tea was good and cold she had Lily decked out in a dozen risqué outfits guaranteed to raise temperatures and spur imagination, despite what little they left to it. Lily wondered if she'd have the nerve to wear some of them, but she was grateful for the instruction, however unwitting, and rather amused to have found an actual use for some of the items cluttering up her closet.

What she didn't like was the buzz about the "hunky" stable hand that her guests seemed to indulge in whenever away from their male compatriots. They spoke of everything from the color of the lock of hair that fell so enticingly across his forehead from time to time to the bulge in his blue jeans and the touch of naughty condescension in his tone and manner.

"That rough-and-tumble sort always give me the shivers," one of the *ladies* commented, leading to bald statements, complete with personal anecdotes, about how, in general, a certain type of common bloke such as the stable hand in question were better lovers than their own kind.

Lily was appalled at such talk—and pulsing green to know that Rollie had provoked such obvious interest among her contemporaries. Had he charmed and flirted with them? Had one or more of her guests slipped out to the stables to sample Rollie's "rough-and-tumble" unbeknownst to her? Would they growl with envy or howl with laughter if they knew what she planned? Much more to the point, what would Rollie do? She meant to find out and soon. In fact, perhaps she ought to consider giving him a taste of what she had just sampled. It would be a calculated risk, of course. One of the conditions her mother had demanded for her frequent solitary visits to the stables was that Lily keep a low profile, relying strictly on Jock and his one or two most trusted ostlers to help her work the horses. But someone there surely knew who she was. She would simply have to trust that he did not dare say so aloud to Rollie. Heaven help her if he found out who she was too soon.

* * *

Certain hours of every day were busy ones in the stable, and such was the case that morning when Lily finally returned. Roland knew something was up almost immediately because of the way that all the usual bustle and activity came to a quick, silent halt. Laying aside the tool he was using to clean a hoof, he straightened and turned to look out into the wide corridor. There, hips swaying with graceful exaggeration, strode Lily, but a Lily unlike any he had seen before.

Gone were the comfortable jeans and classic jodhpurs, the overlarge sweaters and prim blouses. In their place were the tight pants called leggings, which hugged her shape with black, heavily elasticized knit like a jealous lover. To these she had added a pale yellow T-shirt with a deeply scooped neck and the tail tied in a knot beneath her ample breasts, a filmy white shirt that did nothing to hide the obvious and white half boots with stacked heels, the laces conforming the soft leather neatly to her trim ankles. Her hair she had left to fall sleekly about her face and shoulders.

Roland swallowed his heart into place and blinked his eyeballs back into their sockets. He found that he couldn't quite take his gaze off the strip of skin bared by her knotted T-shirt and that it produced pulse-pounding visions of the last time he'd seen her when she'd stood before him all but naked. Suddenly he realized that every other man in the building was looking at her in exactly the same way.

Galvanized into action, he all but busted out of the stall, completely forgetting the tool he'd been using. The gate had not even swung closed behind him when Lily came to a toe-lifting stop in front of him, right in front of him, almost *on top* of him. As if the neckline of that T-shirt didn't reveal enough, she locked her hands behind her back, thrusting the display forward.

"Hello, Rollie."

"Lil—" His voice squeaked to a halt. Clearing his throat, he tried again, this time adopting a low, private tone. "Lily, I—I wasn't expecting you."

She lifted a shoulder, scaring him half to death as it seemed her breast would pop free of its scant covering. "I know I usually come in later, but I've been so busy the last few days and now I have some free time. I just wanted to make a quick check on Lady Doubloon," she said, stepping around him with a twist of her shoulders and another of her hips.

Roland glared at the still-staring workers and turned to follow her. Mistake. The graceful sway of those hips sent his blood pressure spiraling. What on earth did she think she was doing?

She thought, apparently, that she was climbing up on Lady Doubloon's stall gate and making a very public exhibit of herself. He put a stop to that. Curling an arm around her waist, he set her feet right back on the ground. She looked up at him in surprise, batting her pretty eyelashes.

"Why, Rollie, what has gotten into you?"

"Me?" He was violently aware of their audience, even if some of the hands had taken to heart his silent warning and gone back to their duties. He dropped his voice to a murmur. "Where did you get those clothes?"

She blinked, the very picture of innocence, earthy, feral, female innocence just waiting to be stolen. "Out of my closet, of course. Why do you ask?"

"Because they're indecent," he groused.

Lifting her eyebrows in shocked denial, she looked down at herself, then up at him again, one hand planted on a hip that just naturally slid out to accommodate it. "I am quite decently covered, thank you." Her voice lowered to a throaty whisper as she added, "I was wearing a lot less the last time—"

Without thinking, he clapped a hand over her mouth, then just as hastily dropped it and glanced around to see exactly who was watching. Just about everyone, but he put an end to that with a glare meant to peel away the hide of anyone foolish enough to ignore it. The place got busy as a beehive. Only then did he turn back to Lily, and with great patience and care fashioned a calm, reasonable tone. "All I meant was, this isn't like you."

She turned and folded her arms across the top of the gate, propping her chin atop them and cutting her eyes at him. "So you think you know everything there is to know about me, hmm?"

"I didn't say that."

She turned her gaze on Lady Doubloon. "What's wrong with my clothes?"

He clapped a hand to the back of his neck. "Well..." He flattened his mouth, knowing perfectly well that he must choose his words carefully. He didn't dare just blurt that those clothes made her the target of every pair of male eyes within sight. That might make him sound jealous, which he was, but torture couldn't make him admit it. "Nothing," he finally said through his teeth. "They just don't seem your style."

"Oh? And what would my style be, do you think? Staid, dowdy, unimaginative? Proper?"

"Classic," he said flatly.

She whirled and put her back to the gate. "And you know classic styles, do you, Rollie?"

He opened his mouth, thought better of what he was about to say, and closed it again. He was digging a hole here, and since trouble would undoubtedly fill it, let it be a shallow one. Moving to stand beside her, he hooked his elbows over the top of the gate and studied the horse inside the stall.

"Our Lady Doubloon could use a good workout," he said, and Lily tossed back her long, golden hair as she turned her face up to his. "She...*we* have been wondering where you were."

Lily's smile could have lit cities. "Do you have time to take her out now?"

He didn't, and he shouldn't, any more than he should have let her know that he'd been missing her. But what the heck? She looked so happy in that moment, happy and breathtakingly beautiful. He discovered that he was more prone to foolish behavior than he'd realized. "Sure. Why not?"

He didn't even bother to clear it with Jock, just fetched the tack and saddled a dappled gelding for himself while Lily rigged out the mare. When they galloped out of the stable yard, laughing for the sheer joy of it, he was very aware that payment would be required for this bit of folly and that he couldn't have cared less.

They rode for hours and climbed down to sit beneath a majestic elm, their backs to the massive trunk, leafy branches waving overhead in the gentlest of breezes. That breeze carried the tang of the sea with it, a clean, salty, mysterious perfume. It was easy to forget sometimes that they were on an island, but not today. That breeze meant to remind them that they were surrounded by the strength and breadth of the ocean. Lily laid her head back against the rough bark of the tree with a sigh of utter contentment. So far, so good.

After a time, Rollie picked up a twig and began breaking it into tiny pieces which he tossed away one after the other. Lily smiled to herself, delighted with his display of jealousy this morning. He might as well have snarled at his poor coworkers, and he'd swept her out of there with the very first opening she'd given him.

Sitting forward, she drew up her knees and propped her elbows atop them. "You know, I've been thinking."

"About?"

"This ranch of yours."

He turned a bemused expression on her. "What about it?"

"I should think it would be very expensive to get started."

"Very," he admitted, clearly wondering where she was going with this. She didn't keep him in suspense.

"Have you considered taking in investors?"

His eyebrows went straight up. "Investors?"

"I'm sure that Jock would vouch for you," she went on, "and I personally know several people for whom that would be quite sufficient. In fact, I have a little money myself, and my parents, once they get to know you, I'm sure they would want to back you, too."

"Lily!" he exclaimed. "Do you really think I'd let you give me money?"

She lifted her chin imperiously, then quickly lowered it again, remembering her role. "I have as much right to make investments as anyone else."

He chuckled, one hand coming up to stroke her cheek. "Sweetheart, I am deeply touched, but I couldn't let you do that."

"And why not?"

"Because I want to do this on my own."

"But you can't possibly have the funds—"

"Can't I?" he interrupted, slanting a finger across her lips. "I may be just a stable hand, Lily, but I'm not without connections." He took his hand away and squinted out across the meadow. "In fact," he said, "my brother has already offered to bankroll me if I should need him to."

"He's the one in construction," Lily murmured.

"Mm-hmm."

She linked her hands together around her knees, thinking this through and not understanding the implications. "I have to ask you something then," she ventured timidly, taking his glance as permission to go on. "What are you doing here?"

Something indecipherable flashed in his eyes, but then he moved a hand in an exaggerated wave. "Well, you're right about Jock, you know. I, um, wanted to prove myself to him and perhaps even learn a little something from him."

"In other words, you came to study at the feet of the great Jock Browning?" she asked dubiously, echoing the conversation she'd had earlier with Jock.

He opened his mouth, and she saw the lie there, knew that it was right on the tip of his tongue. On the one hand, she was thrilled to realize that she had come to know him so well; on the other hand, she very much feared that she might not know him well enough, after all. But then the lie seemed to dissolve before her very eyes. He shook his head and averted his gaze once more, tossing away the remnants of his twig. "No," he said, "that's not why I came here."

She waited, but he said nothing more. "Even if I pressed you, you wouldn't tell me, would you?"

Glumly, he shook his head. She supposed that she ought to be alarmed, that she ought, even, to be angry, but somehow she couldn't muster that emotion. Looking at him with some surprise, she understood quite clearly in that moment that she loved him. She truly loved him. It wasn't merely a matter of possibilities, of newly awakened desires. It was love, pure and simple. And she saw only one pathway open to her. Trust. She'd just have to trust him.

Pulling a deep breath, she said, "Well, I suppose I'd best not ask then."

Abruptly, he threw his head back, whispering, "Lily!" and then he reached for her.

When he kissed her this time, he kept it light and filled it with gratitude, despite the yearning that she sensed and delighted in. She fought the urge to push for more, to try her newly discovered wiles on this man who was so much more than anyone had dreamed. But though time was short, this was not the moment, and she knew that as well as she knew her own name, which was more than he knew, poor man. Oddly, she felt a little better now about the secret she was keeping from him. He kept his secrets, too, for good reason, surely. He would understand why she had kept hers. Love could cover a multitude of sins, or so she was told. If only time was not slipping away so quickly. She could feel it, slipping through her fingers like water through a sieve, and the only way she knew to hold on to it was to hold on to the man with every means in her power.

Neither of them saw the lone horseman watching from a distance. He waited until they broke the kiss and even then he only moved into the tree line, watching until they finally climbed back into their saddles and cantered away in the direction of the stables. Had they seen him, both would have had reason to fear that all their secrets were coming undone.

Chapter Seven

"I don't want another party."

"Oh, come now," Damon said. "We'll do better than last time, much better. I'll get on the phone and scare up a few dozen more guests. We'll get the orchestra out. They were splendid at the opera recently, by the way. You really should have gone with us. We'll make it a real, old-fashioned ball. You missed all those at the coronation celebration, after all. I still think it was wrong of our parents to forbid you to attend."

"It's all right," she muttered absently. "I didn't mind. I didn't really want to go anyway."

"They are overprotective of you," Damon went on. "Perhaps too much so. I fear they—*we*—have driven you away from the very ones you ought to be growing close to."

She sputtered a mocking laugh at him. "I don't see *you* growing close to the aristocratic nitwits our parents seem determined to surround us with."

"That's different," he said dismissively, crossing his

long legs and spreading his arms out along the back of her sitting room settee. "I did my duty, found my proper mate."

"And lost her," Lily reminded him gently.

"And have no interest in replacing her," he confirmed with deceptive smoothness. "You have yet to meet your heart's mate, sister mine, and you are not likely to do so cloistered away here in this great castle as if it were a nunnery and you a novitiate. We are going to have ourselves a ball, and you are going to enjoy it. Now, who would you like to see here?"

Lily sighed, knowing that she was defeated. Oh, well. The sooner she gave Damon what he wanted, the sooner she could get out to the stables and get to work on what *she* wanted. She wished she could tell Damon about Rollie, about the kind of man he was, about what he made her feel and want. Damon was wrong about her not having found her heart's mate, but she dared not say so until she and Rollie could stand together, united body and soul. She had no doubt that her family would capitulate, not happily perhaps, but capitulate, nevertheless. They wanted her to be happy, after all, and she just didn't see how that was possible without Rollie Thomas.

Now if only she could make Rollie see that, too.

Roland turned off his cell phone and put it away, clipping it inside the front pocket of his jeans. Another week and all the Montague vacation homes would be thoroughly checked out, with nary a lead, he was sure. If Prince Charles himself was not hiding Victor's daughter, then it was a pretty good bet they were barking up the wrong tree, in which case, he'd have no more reason to stay here mucking out stalls and letting Lily flirt with him. He shook his head, wondering how it had all happened. How had she come to consume so much of his time and thoughts? How, without the slightest notion who he was, had she come to fix her interest in him? Or had she somehow learned his identity? No. He couldn't believe it. She trusted him; she couldn't know he was a Thorton. Lord help him, he could almost believe that she loved him. Was it possible that her loyalty to the Montagues was not so strong that his identity wouldn't destroy those feelings? He wished…

With a sigh, he admitted he didn't know what he wished for where the delectable Lily was concerned. He wanted her—*that* was never in doubt—and he was flattered that the feeling appeared to be so very mutual. But Lily was the sort of woman one married. And he had no intention of getting married. Ever.

Did he?

The very thought sent shivers down his spine, but the thought of walking away from this place and never seeing Lily's angelic face again was somehow worse. One thing was certain, he had to make a decision, and soon. His time here was growing short.

With that thought in mind, he left the low-ceilinged room that had served as home for him these past weeks and descended the narrow stairs into the stable below. He immediately spied Lily. She had climbed up on Lady Doubloon's stall gate again, and this time she was wearing an indecently short skirt of white denim beneath a matching jacket. The knee-high white Western boots did nothing to hide the length of thigh exposed. Someone was going to have to do something about this young lady's attire, and it might as well be him. At least the place wasn't packed with ogling ostlers this time—not counting him, of course.

Quickly crossing the large room, he swept up behind her, firmly grasped the hem of her skirt and yanked both it and her down. She gave a little hop as she landed on the floor and glared up at him. He quickly saw that beneath the jacket she was wearing nothing more than a tube top of bright red elastic that just barely covered all it was supposed to. He'd seen bras that were less revealing. Folding his arms, he told her so.

"What is this fixation you have with my clothing?" she asked, nose in the air.

"I just don't like to see you exposing yourself to the salacious gazes of every man on the island."

"Oh, please. Ninety-nine percent of the men in this country have never even laid eyes on me."

"You know what I mean."

He didn't—couldn't—miss the satisfied little smile that curved her lips even as she tilted her chin and stuck her nose higher in the air. "I don't see what business it is of yours."

"Perhaps none," he admitted reluctantly, "but I still don't like it."

She stepped up to the gate, but this time she merely stacked her hands atop it and parked her chin on her knuckles. "Why not?"

He wouldn't answer that. He didn't dare answer that. "It's beneath you, Lily, to flaunt yourself."

She turned and placed a hand on her hip. "If I'm flaunting myself, you have only *yourself* to blame."

"Me?"

"You know I do it just to make you notice me."

God in heaven knew that her efforts were wasted. "Lily," he said, partly exasperated, partly thrilled, "I *notice* you when you're not even around! I think of you every minute of every day, wondering when I'm going to see you next—and lately how *much* of you I'm going to see!"

She chortled at that.

"It isn't funny," he scolded. "I'm trying to do what's

right, Lily, because I care about you so much, but you're making it damned difficult for me to behave myself.''

''Oh, Rollie,'' she said, her vibrant eyes sweeping his face. ''Why can't you see that you are what's right for me?''

''You don't know all there is to know about me.''

''You don't know all there is to know about me,'' she retorted. ''No one knows everything about another person, at least not until they've been together for years and years. Can't you see how much I want that for the two of us? Think of it, Rollie, all those years to discover all that we are.''

She painted a truly compelling picture, but would she feel the same way once she knew who he really was, how great his deception was? He was completely out of options with her. He either succumbed to the will of his heart and committed himself to a path he had never thought to walk, or he left her, tried to forget her, found a way to imagine his life without her. ''Oh, Lily,'' he said, drawing her to him with one arm, ''what am I going to do with you?''

She slid her arms around his waist and said against the hollow of his throat, ''Want a suggestion?''

He started to laugh. Lily, Lily, wonderful Lily. ''I'll make you a deal,'' he said at length, ''I'll go on noticing where you are—and aren't—every moment of the day if you'll just stop dressing to drive me insane.''

She laid her head back and looked him squarely in the eye. ''No.''

He reeled, literally and figuratively. *''No?''*

She locked her hands in the small of his back and targeted his mouth with a positively molten gaze, saying, ''I live to drive you insane, Rollie Thomas, and I'm not going to stop—ever—because I don't want you to behave, not with me. Can't you be just a little less noble?''

She had him perfectly stymied and was absolutely delighted about it. What else could he do but kiss her? And kiss her. And kiss her.

She knew him well enough to know that he had something on his mind, something important, and that he was working his way up to it. Secretly amused—didn't he understand yet that she'd do anything for him?—Lily folded her hands primly in her lap and waited, trying not to fidget so the hay bale upon which she sat would not scratch the backs of her thighs. These short skirts did have their drawbacks.

Rollie, who sat on the floor next to her feet, one knee drawn up as he twirled a piece of straw, sighed and finally came out with it. "I have to ask you some questions, but I need you not to take them the wrong way and not to ask for details. Can you do that?"

She studied his upturned face, scooping her hair back over one shoulder to insure an unimpeded view. He was deeply troubled; she sensed it. Bending forward slightly, she rubbed a thumb over the crease that had grown between his brows. "What do you need to know?"

He tossed away the straw, slinging it aside as if it had suddenly become distasteful to him. Pulling a deep breath, he scrubbed a hand over the back of his neck and came out with it. "Do you happen to know where Prince Charles is now?"

That was perhaps the very last thing she had expected to hear. It took a moment to marshal her thoughts. "Well, let's see. Oh, he's in Rome, at the Vatican. He and m-my, ah, lady's mother have a standing appointment every year during the month of their wedding anniversary to receive the Pope's blessing on their marriage and reign."

"And you're certain that's where they are now?"

"Absolutely. Yes. Why do you—" She abruptly bit off the remaining words. "Sorry."

"You have nothing to apologize for," he told her. "I, on the other hand—" He never finished that thought, but then he didn't have to.

Lily bit her lip and frowned in concentration. Perhaps she'd promised not to ask, but she'd said nothing about wondering. He shifted his position, and Lily knew that another question was coming. He took his time forming it, but nothing could have prepared her for it.

"Is it possible, do you think, that the Montagues—any member of the family, but Prince Charles in particular—could kidnap someone for any reason whatsoever?"

So stunned was she that for several seconds she could not seem to get her mouth around an answer. The words kept trying to come out, but her mouth only wanted to gape. Finally she got it together. "No! Never! How on earth could you even ask such a thing?"

He shook his head. "It's important, Lily. I have to know."

"And I've told you. Never! Not any of them. Why would you—"

"I can't answer that, Lily," he said, rubbing a hand over his face. "Please don't ask."

She studied him for a long time, questions and possibilities whirling through her head until finally they coalesced into something understandable. "You're an investigator of some sort, aren't you? That's why you're here."

He turned his head away. "I wanted to tell you, but I couldn't. I still can't. I would if I could, but it's impossible. An innocent woman's life depends on it, and that's all I can say."

"I should have known!" she exclaimed, more to herself than him. "And perhaps I did." She looked at him again, really looked at him, and saw so much more than a handsome man with dark hair and startling blue eyes. She'd sensed it from the beginning, that Rollie Thomas was more than a mere stable hand, more than a dreamer with big plans, more than a charming, intelligent, talented hand with a horse. She saw more than she'd ever seen before and wanted it all, desperately, but first she had to know something.

"You don't really suspect the Montagues of doing anything so dreadful as kidnapping someone, do you?"

He took a deep breath, and then he shook his head, finally turning his gaze back to hers. "No. No, I don't. Not really. But I had to be sure."

"And are you?"

"I am, yes."

"Can I ask what made you suspect them in the first place?"

"You can ask, but I can't tell you. Suffice it to say, we were grasping at straws from the beginning."

Lily took a deep breath. Grasping at straws. That sounded rather desperate and not too condemning of her family. An innocent woman, he had said. A kidnapping.

"So what happens now?"

He shrugged. "I wait. For another lead to come up."

"Who is she, Rollie?"

For several seconds he said nothing, and then he answered softly, "My half-sister."

She laid a hand on his shoulder. "Oh, Rollie, I'm so sorry."

"Don't ask anything else, please. I can't tell you any more. I can't even tell you what led me here. I shouldn't have said this much."

"I understand."

"You won't say anything to anyone else?"

"No one. I swear it."

He covered her hand with his own, squeezing it against his shoulder. "Thank you."

Another thought occurred to her. "You'll be leaving, won't you?"

"Not immediately," he said, picking up her hand and enfolding it in his larger one. "I don't really have anywhere else to go right now, and this is as good a place as any to wait for more news."

Suddenly she understood that time was much shorter than she had even imagined. Whatever had brought him here, whatever had made him suspect that her family could be behind this atrocity, didn't really seem to matter at the moment. Later, perhaps, she would find whatever it took to be angry about it, but for now she was overwhelmed by two more important factors—his pain and helplessness in the face of this dreadful situation, and her own impending sense of loss. She gripped his hand tightly.

"I'm so sorry, Rollie. I wish I could help you somehow."

"You have helped," he told her, squeezing her hand, "more than you'll ever know."

"But it isn't enough," she said powerlessly, "and you'll be leaving soon."

He didn't deny it. Instead, he stroked her hand with both of his and then carefully, gently set it aside. He got up, dusting the seat of his jeans with one hand, and propped one upraised boot on the hay bale next to her. "I should have told you in the beginning why I came here. I—I just didn't know whom to trust."

"I hope you'll tell me the whole of it before... someday."

"If you like," he said. "When she's safe."

Lily bowed her head. "I can't bear the thought of your going."

"I'm not gone yet."

"Would you..." She bit her lip. "Would you stay if you could?"

He smoothed a hand over her hair. "I'd take you with me if I could."

"But you can't," she surmised in a near whisper, begging him with her eyes to deny it. When he said nothing, merely looked away, she swallowed the tears lumping in the back of her throat. "Is there someone else?"

"No." He cupped her face with his hands. "No."

She nodded, deeply relieved. She hadn't really believed he'd given his heart elsewhere, but such drastic steps as she was now planning demanded some care. Rising smoothly, she stepped forward and slid her arms around his waist. "I mean to convince you to take me with you," she said against his chest, "any way that I can."

"Lily," he whispered. "Oh, my Lily. If I knew that I could give you all that you need and deserve..."

"You can," she assured him, turning her face up to his. "What I need, whether I deserve it or not, is you."

He shook his head. "No man is truly deserving of you, Lily, least of all me. You should have a man who believes in the same kind of love that you do."

"I can teach you to believe," she promised. "Let me teach you to believe."

Groaning, he folded his arms about her and held her close. "If anyone could," he said, "I know it would be you."

If. If. There was her enemy, that doubt. She would find a way to defeat it. Somehow. Somehow.

Roland watched her hurry across the courtyard toward the great house, her hair shining bright in the afternoon sun.

I can teach you to believe. But could she? Could anyone? He bowed his head and massaged his temples with the forefingers of each hand, feeling a headache coming on.

"So, have you told her yet?"

Roland silently groaned at the sound of Jock's voice. Turning, he propped a shoulder against the stone wall of the archway and regarded the wizened little man for whom he had formed a great respect. "Told her what?"

"The truth."

Warily, Roland judged the little man with his gaze, but Jock revealed nothing beyond sheer obstinacy. Two could play that game. "I don't know what you mean."

"No?" Jock shook his grizzled head. "I find that hard to believe."

"You find *what* hard to believe?"

Jock tilted his head. "You haven't even admitted it to yourself, have you?"

Roland folded his arms. "I'm in no mood for riddles, old man."

"Aren't you now? And I wonder why that is? You wouldn't be a wee bit terrified, would you, lad?"

Roland snorted. "Of what?"

"That girl yonder," Jock said with a nod. "You're in love with her, I wager. And I know damned well she's in love with you. What are you going to do about it, now that's my question."

Panic swamped Roland. He forced himself to relax, pretending an insouciance that he was far from feeling. "You don't know what you're talking about, Jock."

"I know a bloody great deal more than you think I do," Jock said with menacing certainty.

Cold dread swept over Roland. "Meaning?"

Jock took a step forward, his hands balled into fists at

his sides. "I didn't know what you were about when you come here," he said flatly. "I still don't, and I don't care to. You want to play stable hand, that's nothing to me. But then our Lily took notice, and I warned you, lad, that I would not allow you to go breaking that lass's heart. Still and all, I want her to be happy, so I stood back and I watched the two of you, and I seen her blossom like the flower she is. And now I'm telling you, you break that lass's heart and I'll see you pay for it, one way or t'other. And I won't be the only one in the performing of that task, I can promise you."

"You think you're man enough to come after me, Jock, you come right on," Roland said evenly, tamping down his anger, "but bring plenty of help."

"You don't know who you're playing with, lad," Jock said. "You just mind that girl's heart, you hear?" With that, the old man turned and stalked away.

Roland sank back against the cold stone wall, shaken and at the same time filled with grudging respect. "And who's going to watch over my heart, old man?" he asked softly.

But it was too late for that, much too late, and Jock was right—it scared the hell out of him. Still and all, he wouldn't be told what he must and must not do by some leprechaun of a stable master. He was royalty, dammit, and mighty sick of being told how to live his life in the first place. When he was done here, his life, by God, was going to be his own, whatever it took, but that was all he really knew about his future. Oh, he meant to have that ranch, couldn't really see himself doing anything else, but for the first time that didn't seem quite enough. *I can teach you to believe.* Maybe that was exactly what he needed. But what if it didn't work out? What if, as time went on, he found himself pulling away, feeling confined and controlled, bored, resentful? What then? He wanted to think that he wouldn't do what his father had done, that he wouldn't slink off to secretly betray the woman who had shared her ability to believe in love with him. But was not indifference itself a kind of betrayal? How many years had he watched his mother deal with his father's coldness? How many times had he sensed the turmoil and disappointment beneath her cool façade? This latest crisis was just another in a long line of difficulties his mother had endured at his father's hands. Perhaps his father's desperation made it so.

Roland didn't want to be like that, to feel like that. Lily would be the one to suffer if it happened. What about Lily's heart then? Who would be there to defend and protect Lily then? Could he trust himself to do it? Could he pretend what he had ceased to feel for her sake?

He didn't know what to think anymore, but he did know that he was afraid to believe in love. It did his ego no good to face the truth about himself, but there it was. Now the question was if he was more afraid of not believing.

It was over. Prince Charles had been exactly where Lily said he was, and now the monarch was on his way back to Roxbury after a stopover in London. Not one iota of evidence linking the Montagues with the kidnapped Thorton had surfaced. None of the information Roland had been able to come up with had yielded even the slightest clue about his sister's whereabouts. His time in Roxbury had served only one purpose: It had confused him in ways he'd never suspected possible. He didn't know what he wanted anymore or even who he was, let alone what he believed. And the worst part was that he had failed his sister and the rest of the family. Perhaps that was why he felt he was about to fail Lily, too, even though he'd made her no promises and had, in fact, been brutally honest about what she could expect from him. At least he'd been honest about *something.*

He pulled his duffle from beneath the narrow bed and unzipped it, suddenly anxious to have his undercover mission over with. He could simply pack and go, just pack his kit and walk away without a word to anyone. He pulled open a drawer and stood looking down at the meager contents, but he wasn't seeing socks and underwear. He was seeing Lily's face. Lily wouldn't merely be upset if he disappeared; she would be crushed. She would feel disappointed, betrayed. But perhaps it was best that way. For him. He bowed his head, ashamed to admit the truth to himself. To tell Lily goodbye, to walk away and actually leave her standing there with her heart in her eyes, well, it would be just unbearable. But to do otherwise would be worse than cowardly.

Roland slammed the drawer, then dropped the empty duffle to the floor and kicked it under the bed. Suddenly exhausted, he sat on the edge of the bed and lay back, arms folded behind his head. He couldn't sneak away, and walking away promised to be the worst sort of torture, and yet, any other course seemed...risky. Frightening. Terrifying.

Lord, was he really thinking about marrying that girl? His parents would very likely have a fit, but what should that matter? He had been the dutiful son; he had stayed home and taken on duties onerous to him while his brother, the heir, had escaped to a new life in America.

Roland figured that it was his turn. His parents were not likely to be happy about his planned exit from family concerns; they might as well be unhappy about having a commoner for a daughter-in-law. The real question was how Lily would feel about having royals for family, especially Thortons.

Perhaps once he told her the truth, her probable revulsion

for the Thortons would solve his problems. Her loyalty to the Montagues was complete, after all, and everyone knew the Montagues hated the Thortons. Once she knew his identity, she was likely to be the one doing the walking. That, then, was the solution—except that the very idea of Lily hating him caused a knot in his belly that just seemed to tighten and tighten and tighten. And what if the miracle occurred and she was somehow able to overlook the lie? What then?

It was over for him here, and yet it wasn't. True, he had no more reason to stay, but surely a day or two more would make no difference. It wasn't as if he could race off to free his sister, after all. He could only wait and hope with the rest of the family, except he could wait better and perhaps even hope better here. With Lily. And in the meantime he would think this thing through and decide once and for all how to handle his departure.

He lay looking up at the low, beamed ceiling for a long while before it occurred to him that he wasn't thinking at all. Disgusted with himself, he pushed up off the bed and went to stand in front of the small, cloudy mirror that hung over the tiny bureau. He looked into his own face, his own eyes, and he knew that he'd already made his decision.

He would tell Lily who he was, and then, if she was still willing, he was going to take her with him, claim her loyalty and her heart for his own, let her teach him what she could, and do whatever it took to make certain that her own faith in the power and truth of love never wavered. Whatever it took.

Lily smiled noncomittally at the demure dress offered by the designer summoned for her and her guests by Damon. The dress was classic, but her purpose was clandestine. Her choice was important, but try as she might, she could not muster the enthusiasm for the process that was exhibited by her companions. Hers was a more clinical approach; too much was at stake to make the choice lightly. Much depended on this dress and how she wore it.

"Oh, I adore it," one of the ladies gushed over the dress in question. "Perhaps you'd like me to try it on for you, Your Highness?"

Lily mustered another insincere smile. "I don't think the color would suit me. In fact, I think it would suit you better." That brought a sigh of delight, and the designer immediately turned his attention to the possible sale. Once a deal had been struck—and never let it be said that the nobility could not bargain—the trunk show continued. The process took hours, but eventually Lily purchased a strapless sarong of muted gold silk with a narrow, draped train and a split skirt—very sexy, very sophisticated and obviously intended for one of the other women. Clearly confused, the designer nevertheless packed up the flounces and hoops and girlish ruffles that were Lily's usual uninspired choices and disappeared, considerably plumper in the pocket.

Lily smiled and pretended gracious interest in the ball, letting her position as the highest ranking member of the party insulate her from the almost giddy excitement of the others. They were plotting entrances and planning fancy dance patterns. She was plotting exits and planning seduction. They were deducing the effects of certain poses and dance steps on their chosen gowns; she was measuring the effect of her gown on her chosen man.

As the castle began to bustle with the arrival of extra wait staff and a full dozen musicians, Lily sent her ladies away to dress. The place already brimmed with flowers and food and champagne. The black-and-white ballroom floor had been polished to a high sheen. The crystal chandeliers blazed with diamond brightness. All around her, excitement bubbled, but Lily felt only desperation. What if Rollie turned her away? What if he didn't, but the loving was not enough to keep him? Was she insane to think him too honorable to walk away from her once she had given herself to him fully?

Doubts and fears assailed her, but she simply couldn't let him walk away without doing everything in her power to keep him. She had almost done as much for a far less worthy reason, and that had overshadowed her life for years. Perhaps she courted disaster this night, but disaster was at hand anyway. What part of the years ahead would not be a disaster if the love of her life walked away without a backward glance? Why sit passively and let it overtake her? She had to do something. She had to fight with the only weapons available to her—love and desire. If she failed, as well she might, then at least she would have tried. For once since her sixteenth summer, she would be brave enough to try to wrest from life what she truly wanted. It was time for the princess to stop being a victim and start being a woman.

Chapter Eight

She came to him as if in a dream, gilt all golden by the moonlight spilling through his uncurtained window and the luster of things desired but not hoped for. Cocooned in silk and crowned in starlight that seemed to wisp about her face, she clutched two flutes and a bottle of champagne in her gloved hands. He lay upon his narrow bed, certain she couldn't be real, until the door clicked shut very audibly behind her. He jackknifed up into a sitting position.

"Lily?"

"You were expecting someone else?" she asked in a throaty voice that seemed to tremble with a mixture of excitement and trepidation.

He didn't bother to answer that, still not quite believing what he saw. She looked like a cross between Veronica Lake and Aphrodite in that dress, her hair piled artfully atop her head to expose the slender length of her neck and the pale slopes of her bare shoulders, not to mention the diamonds that hung in sparkles from her dainty earlobes and the center of a delicate chain that encircled the base of her throat. Lower, much lower, the dress draped and wrapped all the way to the floor and then some, trailing after her in a slither of silk as she walked toward him, displaying a long, creamy length of slender leg on shoes that with every step seemed little more than tall, spiky heels. The bodice just barely covered what it was meant to, propping everything above the dark peach aureoles of her nipples into a display of womanly plumpness that literally made his mouth water. He remembered so well the look of those bared breasts, the feel of them in his hands. He had imagined their taste a hundred—a thousand—times. Something told him he wouldn't have to rely on his imagination any longer.

He sat back against the headboard, the pillow scrunched behind him, and drew up one knee to hide what was taking place beneath the covers.

"Where in heaven's name did you get that dress?"

She turned aside and placed the champagne glasses on the rickety bedside table. "Does it matter?"

It might have, but he'd already forgotten the question. He watched her fill the glasses with the sparkling champagne, and a new one came to mind. "Where did you get the bottle?"

"I stole it." She turned a teasing smile on him and held out a glass. His gaze traveled up her gloved fingers, past her wrist, over her slender forearm, beyond her elbow and on to where the glove finally ended. Mechanically, somehow fascinated by the glove, literally dozens of which he'd seen in his lifetime, Roland took the glass.

"What shall we drink to?"

"To tonight," she replied huskily, clinking her glass with his.

Tonight. He had little doubt why she had come, or what it would mean. Expectation sizzled along his nerve endings.

"To tonight," he said, lifting his gaze to hers, "and tomorrow."

Her smile was soft and filled with such promise that it fairly took his breath away. The hardness snaking against his thigh suddenly rose against his belly, stiff as stone. He lifted his glass toward his mouth but somehow never got it there as he watched Lily empty her own. She let her head fall back, tilting the glass until all the pale amber liquid had poured down her gently working throat. When she was done, she set the glass on the table once more and wiped her mouth with the back of her hand. Roland's throat went dry, and he took a quick gulp of the bubbly brew, avid to see what she would do next. She certainly didn't disappoint.

Purposefully working one finger at a time, she used her small, white teeth to loosen her glove, and then peeled it down her arm and let it fall to the floor. Roland's breath hitched, but he sipped more champagne to hide it, eyes wide over the brim of his glass. With her bare hand, Lily reached up and gently plucked the baubles from her earlobes, turning her head side to side in order to reach them. These, too, she left atop the small, battered table, drops of starlight against the base of the bottle. Twisting slightly, she perched a hip on the side of his bed and crossed her legs, essentially baring them as the skirt fell away from the slit in its side. His hand naturally fell upon her knee. The warmth of her flesh radiated through the cool, sleek silk of her stocking.

"Drink your champagne," she instructed in a low, smoky voice that made him think of banked fires.

Obediently, he sipped from his glass, while she kicked off one shoe and eased her skirt higher in order to expose the white, lace-edged strap of a garter, which she released. Lifting her foot to the edge of the bed, she reached behind her leg for the second garter and released it as well. Then carefully, with agonizing slowness, she hooked the thumbs of both hands, one yet gloved, in the top of her stocking and slid it down her leg to her ankle. Flexing her foot, she stripped the stocking free and tossed it over her shoulder.

Roland felt a ridiculously wide grin stretch his mouth at that bit of flamboyance. He could hardly wait to see her strip off the other stocking. To his surprise, she stood for this, and lifted her foot to the bed, digging her spiked heel into the mattress. The expression on her face seemed to ask if he would help poor little old her as she had completely exhausted herself with that other stocking. Eagerly, he placed his champagne on the table and reached for her foot. Slipping off the shoe, which was as light as a feather and seemed constructed wholly of some transparent acrylic, he tossed it over his shoulder as she had done with the stocking. It *clunked* against the wall and fell into the corner behind the bed.

Lily threw back her head and laughed, the sound floating up from deep in her throat. He chuckled, too—until she reached into the slit of her skirt and swept it back, bunching it beneath her bottom and exposing the garter to his trembling fingers. He slipped the first one, and she leaned into the bed, knee bent, so that he could reach around her for the second. When that one was free, she straightened again, presenting him with the whole, smooth length of her slender leg. He splayed his hands lightly around the top of the hose and slowly slipped it down her leg. When he reached her foot, he lifted it in one hand and plucked the stocking free with the other, leaving it where it fell upon the bed. He reached for her then, but she placed her foot in the center of his chest and pushed him back.

"My turn," she said, straightening, and before he could guess what she meant to do, she reached down and grasped the edge of the bed covers, tossing them aside. Inanely, he grappled to cover himself, embarrassed by both the sudden exposure and his own reaction to it. Momentary shock widened Lily's expressive eyes, but then she hitched an eyebrow upward and visibly relaxed. "I didn't realize you slept in the nude."

He made himself ease back into a semi-reclining position. Her eyes widened again at the sight of his straining erection. "Now you know," he told her, the words rasping in his throat.

"Now I know," she said breathlessly, sinking down onto the side of the bed once more. She looked him over quite openly, her curiosity both obvious and precious, and where she looked, her hands followed.

She began with his shoulders and chest, skimming them with one gloved hand and one bare. The contrast, whether she intended it or not, was maddeningly seductive. He forced himself to remain still, to let her explore at the pace that suited her. This was her production; she deserved to be in charge. Whether or not he was going to survive it was another question entirely, but he wouldn't have stopped her for the world.

She moved on to his biceps, stroking them lightly, then transferred her hands to his thighs. He gulped, flinching beneath her touch, and she looked up sharply.

"Is something wrong?"

"Heavens, no. You're killing me, that's all."

"Do you want me to stop?"

"Never!"

Smiling slightly, she switched her gaze and her hands to his belly, flattening her palms against the suddenly drum-taut muscles there. And then she reached for him, curling her bare fingers around his throbbing flesh. His eyes rolled back in his head. Ecstasy. Torturous ecstasy. She clutched him tightly, and then began to stroke him lightly with her gloved hand. He couldn't seem to get enough air, though his lungs were pumping like bellows. If this sweet agony continued a moment longer, he was going to embarrass himself, and disappoint her, terribly. But before he could make himself say so, he felt her weight shift and her hands fall away.

He opened his eyes to find her on her knees, straddling his thighs.

"I love you, Rollie," she whispered, and it seemed suddenly as if his heart might burst from his chest.

Tell her now, his conscience commanded. *Tell her who and what you are, before it's too late.*

Love her first, his heart argued. *Tell her afterward, when you are bound, body and soul.*

Trust her love, his mind said, *and your own.*

He opened his mouth, but she covered it with her gloved hand. "Don't say it," she pleaded. "I want you to show me."

He smiled against the palm of her gloved hand. What a wise and wonderful woman she was. Had he really thought of leaving her? Had he really doubted that this was right? He was going to show her, all right. He was going to show her everything she needed to know about loving and being loved, and then he was going to tell her the truth and ask her—beg her—to marry him. If somehow she couldn't love a Thorton, well, he'd just spend the rest of his life changing her mind.

Gripping her wrist lightly, he lifted her palm away and then brought the tip of her thumb to his mouth. His eyes on her face, he sank his teeth delicately into the fabric of her glove, just grazing her fingertip. A gentle tug loosened the fabric. He shifted her hand and bit the glove tip of her index finger, mimicking the motions she'd gone through earlier, until the glove was wholly dislodged. Only then did he seize the empty fingertips in one hand and pull the glove slowly from her arm. She followed it, crouching over him on her knees and affording him a magnificent view of her breasts.

His gaze glued to those succulent mounds, he dropped the glove and brought her hand back to his mouth. Gently, he suckled her fingers, one by one, teasing their tips with the edges of his teeth and laving their creases with his tongue. He kissed her palm and bit the heel of her hand, licked her wrist, tasted the hammering pulse, sucking against it. Beneath her bodice, her nipples puckered and swelled. He lifted his free hand to cup her, and with a small cry she threw herself at him, her mouth colliding with his.

What she lacked in expertise she more than made up for in enthusiasm. Needing to hold her still in order to deepen the kiss, he brought his hands to her head and plunged them into her hair, scattering pins as silken tresses tumbled free. He stabbed his tongue into her mouth, forcing her jaws wide to accept his invasion, and seizing her at the waist, he pulled her astride his lap. He attempted to shove down the bodice, but it was too tight. He reached for the center of her back, but found nothing to help him free her. Moaning against his mouth, she lifted one arm, and he fumbled for the zipper there, dragging it down to her waist and beyond.

Loosened, the bodice gaped. He shoved it down and filled his hands, lifting himself against the apex of her spread thighs at the same time. Crying out, she let her head fall back, breaking the kiss, and the moment he had dreamed of since first seeing this luscious bounty bared was at hand. Wrapping an arm around her waist, he hauled her higher and bent his head to fill his mouth with peaches.

He suckled her fiercely, rimming her pebbled nipple with his teeth and then taking as much of her into his mouth as he could. He felt her push her pelvis against him, and when he slipped his hand between them, he found her not only bare but wet and eager. He had to smile. Last time she had dropped her dress and stood before him in nothing but her panties. This time she was leaving nothing to chance. She didn't have a blasted thing on under that dress but a garter belt, and he intended for that to hit the floor momentarily, right after the dress itself.

Meanwhile she was panting as if he'd chased her through every room on every floor of the great house across the way. He moved his fingers, eliciting tiny cries from her, and he pulled his mouth from her breast, intending to move to the other, when the door slammed open and a man stepped into the room.

Instinctively, Roland shoved Lily to the side and rolled from beneath her, his feet hitting the floor even as he stretched out one arm to protect her and made a grab for the covers with the other. The lamp atop the bureau beside the door snapped on.

"What the hell do you think you're doing?" the man roared. Roland managed to get to his feet before the man spoke again. "You get out of that bed this instant, Mary Louise Lillian Eugenie!"

Mary Louise? Lillian Eugenie? *Lillian?* The meaning of that hit at the same instant that Roland realized the identity of the man standing in his room. Prince Damon. His head rotated slowly to the woman on his bed.

And Princess Lillian, no doubt.

Groaning, Roland sat down again on the edge of the bed, hard, a hand going to his head. His Lily *was* the princess! That was Lillian Montague wrenching up her bodice and glaring at her brother from his bed. Lily! No commoner at all, no lady's maid in the home of the enemy, but the enemy herself! Suddenly the dress, the diamonds, the parties, the naming of Lady Doubloon—all spelled the same glaring truth. Idiot! He was a flaming idiot! How could he not have known? Because she had lied, that was how.

Lily—*Lillian*—had scrambled off the bed and was struggling with her zipper while kicking at her skirt. "How dare you burst in here like that, Damon?"

"How dare *I?* Have you lost your mind? Bedding down with a stable hand! The man's a fortune hunter, Lil!"

"He is not!"

"I am not!"

"You should know better," Damon went on angrily. "We've covered this ground before, five years ago when—"

"I'm not a child anymore, Damon!" Lily exclaimed in her haughtiest princess-of-the-realm voice. "It's time I started to live my own life. I love Rollie and he—"

"We'll see about that." Stepping toward Roland, Damon whipped a wad of bills from the breast pocket of his expertly tailored black tuxedo jacket. Obviously, he had come prepared. "How much to escape without a beating? One thousand? Two thousand? Three?" As he spoke, he peeled bills from the sheaf in his hand.

Roland had, quite literally, had enough. Clutching the sheet wrapped around his hips with one hand, he rose to his feet and slapped the bills from Damon's hand with the other. "I am *not* a fortune hunter."

"He's not a stable hand, either," Lily proclaimed. "He's a rancher."

"I am not a rancher," Roland said, "yet."

"He's a private investigator, too," Lily plunged on. "He's—"

"*Not* a private investigator!" Roland snapped.

"Looking for his sister," Lily finished.

"Here?" Damon sneered. "He's looking for his sister here? Where? Beneath your skirts?"

Roland lost it. He felt heat surge upward from his chest and explode out the top of his head. "I am Roland George Albert Thomas Thorton of Thortonburg!" he roared. "And if you speak to her like that again, you'll be speaking out of your ear the next time you open your mouth!"

Shocked silence followed that diplomatic announcement. Damon slowly tilted his head, looking Roland over very carefully. Finally, he frowned, his mouth flattening to a thin line.

"I knew I recognized you," he muttered. "But who could expect to find a damned Thorton mucking out the stables?"

"Thorton?" Lily echoed, as if only then recognizing the name. She shook her head, arms crossing protectively over her chest. "No, that's not possible. He—"

"Lied," Roland interrupted icily. "The same as you, *Your Highness.*"

"B-but—"

"How else was I to get myself employed here?" Roland demanded, still smarting from her deception. "How else was I to learn what I had to?"

Lily's eyes shimmered with tears. "Th-Thorton," she said. "You came here to spy on us!"

"I came here to look for clues to my sister's disappearance," he insisted less hotly.

"You used me!" she accused. "All those questions! You used me to f-find out..."

He couldn't deny it. "I had to know," he argued. "It wasn't as if I had a choice."

Tears began to spill down her cheeks. "How could you? How *could* you?"

"I was going to tell you," he said, starting to feel desperate now.

"When?" she demanded caustically. "In the morning?"

"Yes. When I asked you to marry me."

She laughed at that, scrubbing tears from her face with her knuckles. "You expect me to believe that you were going to ask a lady's maid to marry you, *Prince Roland of Thortonburg?*"

"That's exactly what I was going to do," he said softly. "Now, I'm asking a princess."

"A Thorton?" she asked scathingly. "You suspected us of kidnapping! You tried to use me to prove—"

"No." He shook his head. "I needed information, but I told you, we were grasping at straws, looking for any reason for what has happened."

"And it just stands to reason that the Montagues are responsible!" she cried. "Oh, God, what have I done?"

Turning, she fled from the room in her bare feet, tears streaming down her face, hair tumbled wildly.

"Lily!" He bolted after her, only to be yanked up short when Damon stepped on the tail of his sheet. Roland turned to glare at the other man, then he dropped the sheet and lunged toward the bureau. Snatching open a drawer, he grabbed a pair of jeans and began dragging them on, hopping from foot to foot.

Damon calmly stepped over to the door and closed it, leaning against it with his arms crossed.

"Get out of my way."

"No."

"Dammit! She needs me. She—"

"I think you've done quite enough for her for one night."

"You don't understand what's going on here. Lily loves me, and I love her."

"Do tell?"

"Damn you! Do you think she'd have come to my room like this if she didn't love me?"

"I think," Damon said with maddening composure, "that you'd better tell me exactly what you're doing here—besides the obvious, of course."

"Can't this wait?" Roland demanded, pushing a hand through his hair.

"If you're Roland Thorton," Damon went on doggedly, "and I've no doubt that you are, then you cannot possibly be looking for your sister because you don't have one."

Roland sighed inwardly. Heaven help him, what a mess! He shook his head. "I did come looking for my sister," he said desperately, "my *half*-sister. We didn't know she existed until a few weeks ago."

"That's preposterous."

"My father had an affair," Roland announced baldly, "well before I was born. She's a year older than me and undoubtedly my half-sister, but he didn't even know she existed until we received the ransom note during the coronation celebration at Wynborough."

"Good God, man."

Roland looked at the closed door. Lily was out there, believing the worst of him—and here he stood about to increase the feud between their families because he had to know the truth. If only his family were not depending on him, if only he could be sure Damon would tell him what he needed to know *after* he convinced Lily to marry him, for he had to. He knew that now without the least doubt. Lily—Lillian—Montague was made for him, only for him, and he couldn't believe that he hadn't realized as much from the moment he'd first laid eyes on her. Lady's maid or princess, she belonged with him. But his sister belonged with her family, not in the clutches of some kidnapper. He closed his eyes briefly and made the only decision he could. Impatiently, tersely, he drilled Damon for information.

"Do you know something about my sister's disappearance? Lily had convinced me that the Montagues could not be involved, but so help me, Damon, if you know something about this kidnapping, I'll beat it out of you if I have to."

"I know the relationship between our families has been strained to say the least," Damon began, "but on my honor—not just as a man but as a brother—I give you my word the Montagues know nothing of your sister's whereabouts, nor would we harm any member of your family."

Roland saw the truth in Damon's eyes and knew the Montague lead was a dead end. He extended his hand, an offering of peace and said, "I believe you."

Damon accepted Roland's handshake, a fragile truce forming between the men.

Then Roland ended their grip, wrenched open the door, daring the other man with a look to try and stop him. "I'm going to find your sister. And I'm warning you now, I mean to marry her."

"We'll see about that," Damon said coolly. He nodded at Roland's bare chest and added, "You might consider at least putting on a shirt."

Roland grimaced and stalked over to the closet, where he ripped a fresh shirt from a hanger and threw it on. Just for good measure, he stomped his bare feet into his boots, all the while eying Damon.

"Off to the wars then, are we?"

"Don't try to stop me," Roland warned.

"Wouldn't dream of it, old boy," Damon said with irritating glee. "Shouldn't think I'll have to actually. You've only met Lily, the stable haunt. Princess Lillian is another entity altogether. The men my parents keep throwing at her head call her the Ice Princess. I think you'll soon see why."

"You're wrong," Roland said implacably. "Princess or maid, she belongs with me, and she knows it."

"And just how do you expect our respective families to feel about it?"

That gave Roland pause. Good God, the idea of a commoner would have been bad enough as far as his parents were concerned. His father was likely to have an apoplectic fit when told he was going to have a hated Montague for a daughter-in-law! He imagined that Charles Montague would react in a similar manner.

Well, so be it. Lily the lady's maid or Princess Mary Louise Lillian Eugenie Montague—one thing he'd known for dead certainty the moment he'd seen his dream materialize right before his eyes was that she'd already taught his reluctant heart to believe with a faith previously foreign to it that true love did exist. In her. For him only in her. He'd been a fool to think he could ever walk away. More the fool was he who tried to stand between them.

He looked Damon straight in the eye and said, "I don't give a good damn how any of you feel about it. Lily is mine. Whatever it takes."

Catching the door frame with one hand, he swung out of the room. As he jogged down the hall, he could almost have sworn that he heard Damon Montague chuckling sympathetically behind him.

They weren't having a party at the castle this night, they were having a full-fledged ball! So when Roland arrived in his jeans, boots and shirt with the tail hanging loose, the formally costumed footmen promptly threw him out. After he went back and revealed his identity, they threw him out and laughed at him, saying that the princess herself had warned them that the stable hand had lost his mind. After he demanded that they ask Princess Lillian to personally confirm his identity, they threw him out and threatened to shoot him! His own footmen would have taken bayonets to anyone appearing as he did, but they wouldn't have laughed and jeered and bothered to explain that she had warned them he would claim to be on the lookout for a lady's maid claiming to be royalty. Damon was right. Lily definitely had a cold streak running through all that molten passion, but she had met her match in him. Literally. And she had to know it.

Left with no other option, he stood in the courtyard and proceeded to make a fool of himself, bellowing at the top of his lungs.

"Lily!"

"Lily!"

"Lily!"

Eventually, a few curious faces appeared at various windows, but not the one he was seeking.

"Lily, I have to talk to you!"

"Lillian Montague, show yourself!"

"I need you, Lily! Lily!"

A footman with a ceremonial musket appeared. Roland gave him fair warning with a pointed finger.

"Lily, I don't want to hurt anyone, but I'm not leaving until you talk to me!"

The footman rolled his eyes, but kept his musket shouldered.

"I want to marry you, Lily! I love you, Lily!"

Finally, a light came on in a third-floor window, the window went up, and Lily's golden head appeared.

"Go away, Rollie, before I have you shot!" she yelled.

"I can't," he shouted back, throwing his arms wide. "I love you!"

"You don't believe in love!"

"I do now!"

She shook her head stubbornly. "It was all lies, for both of us."

"No," he said, his voice beginning to sound hoarse. "It was all true in a way."

She shook her head again. "You aren't a stable hand."

"No? What else do you call someone who works in a stable? Just because I'm royalty, too, doesn't mean that the man you know is false."

"But that's the point!" she cried. "We would do better if we were only what we pretended!"

"We are what we are, Lily," he cried, and going down on one knee, he covered his heart with one hand. "Marry me, Lillian Montague!"

She dabbed tears from her eyes and arched her neck out the window, looking down at him. "I can't marry a Thorton! My father—"

"Mine, too!" he bellowed. "It doesn't matter! We'll have each other!"

To his dismay, she burst into tears. "Your parents would disown you!"

"But we would be together!"

"I can't do that to you!" She gripped the window ledge with both hands and looked down at him, her hair sliding about her face and shoulders. "Why couldn't you be Rollie the stable hand?" she sobbed.

"I can," he told her, but the window had already slammed closed. He backed away, confused but determined—and that was when he realized that half the aristocracy in the islands was standing in the courtyard in all their finery, watching him lose the woman he loved. Well, let them watch. He might have lost the battle, but the war was far from over. He drew himself up to his fullest, most regal height and bawled like a general giving orders to his troops. ''I'll be back! Because you, Mary Louise Lillian Eugenie Montague, belong to me!'' He thumped his chest and glared at the crowd clustered around the door. ''Me!'' he declared one last time before turning and walking away. ''Only me.''

Chapter Nine

"Now let me see if I've got this straight," Jock said, scratching his ear. "You were in love with him when he was Rollie the stable hand, but now that he's of your own station, you want nothing to do with him?"

Lily wiped tears from her eyes with her fingers and shook her head. "It's not that simple, Jock. I *can't* love a Thorton!"

"Can't?" Jock echoed disbelievingly. He brought his hands to his hips and glared at her, literally glared, Jock, who had ever been her friend and champion. "Lass, I don't know what to think of you," he said, his voice dripping with disappointment. "After years of living like a shadow, I watched you bloom these past weeks. A blind man could see that it was Rollie doing it. I kept your secret so you'd know it was you he wanted and not what you could bring him. I kept his secret—not that I knew precisely who he was, mind you, but I knew he was more than he let on—because I trusted him and I felt you needed time, the two of you, to come together. Now you're telling me that because his last name is Thorton, you want nothing to do with him?''

Why didn't he understand? Everyone knew that the Montagues and the Thortons despised one another. ''Can you imagine what my father would do if I told him that I was marrying a Thorton?'' she demanded.

''Oh, aye, that I can,'' Jock said complacently. ''Your Pa, he is as predictable as the tides, God bless him. Even as a boy when he didn't get his royal way, he'd puff and strut and make all sorts of edicts he had no intention of enforcing. Then someone, myself usually—which is why I've been threatened more than once with gaol, you understand—would haul him off by his lapels and give him a good talking to, and gradually he'd come around. Your mother, God preserve her, is the one to do the lapel-pulling now, and she's a mite more persuasive than ever I was, I can tell you, having so much more to work with, no doubt. Aye, our Charles can be difficult, but he's not unreasonable.''

''I wish I could be as certain of that as you seem to be,'' Lily told him morosely, ''but I just can't believe it would be that easy. I've already disappointed him once, and—''

''Lass, you took that little folly too much to heart,'' Jock said kindly. ''You were a child with a child's judgment five years ago. No one holds that against you, nor did they ever. I thought, with Rollie, that you were finally beginning to put that behind you, to come into your own as a woman. And now here you are in my stables sniveling like it was five years ago still. I'm sore disappointed, I am, lass.''

''I'm disappointed, too, Jock,'' she insisted petulantly. ''I thought Rollie was the answer to all my prayers.''

''Oh, aye, then the lowly stable hand turned into a highborn royal and ruined all your lovely dreams of...what?

Lording it over him? Pleasing your parents with a commoner for a son-in-law?''

Lily put her hands to her head. Why did he make it sound so silly? Rollie being a Thorton was a big problem, a huge problem, far larger than his having been a stable hand. Although, thinking of it, she knew that she'd been ready and able to endure her father's wrath and her mother's disappointment in marrying beneath her station. But didn't it matter that Rollie had lied to her? That he had used her? That he had suspected the Montagues of such vile activities as kidnapping? Of course, she had lied to him, too, but that was different. Sort of. She had only been protecting herself. She, after all, was the one with the history of betrayal and heartbreak—not that he could have known that. Oh, she was so confused! And miserable, utterly miserable.

That was why she'd come to the stables to see Jock. For so long now this place and this gruff, kindly man had been her only escape from the gilded cage that was her life. He had given her a kind of normalcy that her parents, in their duty-bound roles, could not even comprehend. Now, though, everywhere she looked, she saw only Rollie, and Jock was certainly not helping as he should be.

''I don't know why I even came here,'' she whined, hating the sound of her own voice. ''You seem intent on making me feel as if this fiasco is all my own fault.''

Jock scratched an ear. ''Fault is not something I figure needs assigning in this case,'' he said. ''You both lied for reasons of your own—good reasons, it seems to me. Then the truth comes out, and this so-called enemy of yours opens his arms wide...while you run and hide. Now I'm wondering what it is you're hiding from, lass. Him? Or your own self? Or is it love you're afraid of, lass?''

She shook her head stubbornly. *She* was the true believer. *She* was the one willing to risk all, the one determined to teach Rollie what her own heart had known from the cradle. It wasn't true that she was afraid. Was it? If fear was not what had her heart pounding in panic at the idea of seeing Rollie again, then what was? Suddenly she couldn't bear to be in this place where he had been, to remember all they'd said and done, the smiles and laughter—and kisses. Her gaze swept the shadowy building, looking for her haven, her little universe of faux normalcy, but finding only memories and loss. Without another word, she turned from Jock and ran from this place, feeling as though she had lost her only sanctuary and friend in the whole wide world. And whose fault was that if not Roland Thorton's? Whose fault, indeed.

"Good work," Rafe said, clapping Roland on the shoulder before hurrying to assist his wife as she lowered herself gingerly into an armchair on the other side of the family parlor. Elizabeth was in the final trimester of pregnancy, her vivid auburn hair and green eyes literally glowing with good health and happiness. The look she turned on Rafe as he fussed over her comfort was full of such love that it made the breath catch in Roland's chest. Lily had looked at him like that once, and it had terrified him. Now he was afraid that he might have lost her. But no, he wouldn't let himself think it. He dared not. If he doubted, he would never be able to do what he must this day.

His parents entered the room. Roland was surprised to see that his father, who was usually so careful about public displays, had his arm looped loosely about his wife's trim waist. They had greeted one another at breakfast only an hour ago, but his mother, nevertheless, crossed the room to embrace and kiss him, while Victor waited with arm outstretched as if loath to let her go even for that little moment. Roland smiled a question at his mother, wondering what had changed during his absence, but she merely hurried back to his father and allowed him to seat her on the comfy, overstuffed sofa upholstered in huge bouquets of roses. Victor took a place next to her, his arm draped about her shoulders. Roland mentally shook his head. Whatever it was, he could feel it; a certain aura about the room, a lightness, a brightness. He had felt it at breakfast, too, and been unable to pinpoint it then, either. It was almost as if everyone had relaxed their guards, despite the thick overlay of worry for their kidnapped family member.

Lance Grayson was the last to arrive, one hand pressed to the tiny earpiece of the radio and microphone that he always wore when about the castle. He nodded his head as if listening, a sheaf of papers clutched in his other hand.

After a few seconds he said in a low voice, "Excellent. I'm clear until further notice. Emergencies only." With that, he turned and closed the door to the room, then pushed the microphone wire down before facing them once more and making a perfunctory bow.

"Well," Victor barked. "What news have you?"

Grayson nodded in the direction of the cold fireplace, where Roland stood. "Thanks to the information that Roland was able to get to us, we have been able to exonerate the Montagues of any duplicity in the disappearance of Victor's daughter."

"And what of Maribelle? Have you found her yet, Grayson?" Victor said after a long moment.

"No, Your Grace," Grayson said, "but we continue to investigate all Maribelles in the Grand Duchy, and to examine birth records."

"Do whatever is necessary. *Carte blanche*. Just find my daughter."

"And bring her home," Sara added, laying her hand on

her husband's thigh. Victor covered it with his own and squeezed.

Grayson executed the requisite bows and turned once more to Roland. "My congratulations, sir. Your information has been invaluable. Well done."

Roland inclined his head. The praise seemed largely undeserved to him, but perhaps it would help with the scene to come. "Thank you, Grayson. You will, of course, let me know if I can be of any further assistance?"

"Absolutely."

He made his final bows and quickly left the room, closing the door behind him.

To Roland's everlasting surprise, his father turned his attention to him and declared baldly, "I owe you more than I can say, son. Grayson is right. You've done well. Thank you."

Roland was too stunned to do more than blink and, belatedly, nod.

"I think we're done here," Rafe said. "I'll just take my wife up for a little lie-down now."

"Uh, if you'd be so kind, Rafe," Roland quickly interjected, "I'd appreciate your presence a moment longer. As it happens, I have an important personal announcement to make." His heart began to race, and his palms grew sweaty, but he straightened the line of his suit jacket, shrugging his shoulders to ease the fit, and refused to let it show.

Rafe traded looks with his wife, who slid to the edge of her seat and began levering her weight onto her feet, saying, "Since this is personal, perhaps I should excuse myself."

"No, please," Roland said. "I suspect I'm going to need the calming influence of a neutral party. I'd like you to stay, if that's all right."

Elizabeth lifted an eyebrow at her husband, but then

eased back into her chair. "I don't think I qualify as neutral, but I'll stay if you're sure you want me to."

"Positive."

"My goodness, son, this sounds ominous," Sara commented lightly, just a touch of nervousness in her voice.

Roland smoothed his Italian-silk tie with one hand and forced a smile. "Not at all, Mother, not from my perspective, anyway."

"Perhaps you'd better not keep us in suspense any longer," Rafe prodded. "You say you have an announcement to make?"

Roland nodded and cleared his throat. Funny, but now that the moment was at hand, his heart rate had slowed and his palms were no longer clammy. He knew what was coming, but he also knew that this was right. He belonged with Lily just as Rafe belonged with Elizabeth. That being the case, he simply came out with it. "I'm going to be married."

The room erupted with comment.

"Married, did he say?"

"Was he seeing someone? I didn't know!"

"Married! I don't believe it!"

"But who is the bride?" This last came from his mother, and it was the only question directed to him personally, so he answered it.

He actually grinned, believing himself wholly prepared for what was coming, and said, "Lillian Montague."

"Montague!" his father gasped.

"Lillian?" Elizabeth crowed.

"The princess?" Sara asked in a perplexed tone.

"Well, she's not the lady's maid," Roland said through his teeth, though only he could understand the irony of his words.

"But the Montagues hate us," Sara went on. "Don't they?"

"Of course they do!" Victor growled, frowning.

"Not all of them," Roland corrected. "At least one of them doesn't. Two, actually, I think."

"Damon, you mean," Rafe supplied helpfully.

"Yes. He's a good man, an ally, I think...and this after he'd discovered his sister in my bed," Roland revealed with what he felt was great nonchalance. He had thought long and hard about making such a confession, but he was determined that his parents understand just how serious he was in this, and he could think of no better way than the truth. God knew that his lies had recently risen up to confront him, justifiable as they were.

It was his mother who once again cut to the heart of the matter. "Oh, Roland, you haven't compromised that poor girl, have you?"

He almost chuckled. "No one compromises another anymore, Mother," he said indulgently. "Although, to put your mind at ease, it was Lily who came unexpectedly to my room last night—not that I wasn't willing to, er, be compromised, you understand. However, Damon arrived before any actual, ah, compromising could be done."

"So you're telling us that this marriage is not a necessity," Victor rumbled.

Now the explosion would come, Roland decided. "A necessity, no," Roland said firmly, "a certainty, yes." He hoped.

To Roland's surprise, Victor merely flattened his mouth into a grim line, much as if he'd just tasted something unpleasant.

"Well," Elizabeth exclaimed after a moment, "I think it's wonderful!"

Roland's mouth twitched in a suspicious smile. "It's kind of you to say so."

"No, I mean it," she went on. "How better to put an end to the feud?"

"But will it?" Rafe asked uncertainly.

Roland shrugged. "I don't know, and I don't care, frankly. All that matters to me is that Lily has the support and acceptance that she deserves."

"What about her family?" Sara asked. "Will they accept this marriage?"

Roland took a deep breath. "I think Damon will. I really can't say about her mother. I know she's anxious for both of her children to marry, but whether she'll welcome a Thorton..." He let that thought trail off and addressed himself to another. "Her father I expect to be as intractable and hard-headed as my own."

Victor flashed him an enigmatic look. "Hard-headed perhaps," he admitted in a gravelly voice, "but intractable?" He shook his head. "If I've learned one thing these past weeks, Roland, it's that those who cannot bend, break, and I've too much good in my life to let this, or anything else, break me." As he spoke, he gripped his wife's fair hand in his own much larger one.

Roland felt his jaw begin to descend and fought to keep it clamped. Was it possible that his father had actually changed, softened? He managed to pull together enough sangfroid to ask, almost casually, "Are you saying, sir, that you can tolerate this marriage and accept Lily into the family?"

Victor lifted his chin, and Roland saw in that the shadow of the old Victor. He saw, too, what it cost his father to set that man aside. "You are my son, Roland," Victor said finally. "Over the years you've displayed uncommon good sense and a depth of devotion to family and duty that have made me very proud."

This time Roland's jaw nearly hit the rug. "Sir?" he croaked, uncertain that he'd actually heard what he thought he had.

Victor made an impatient face and launched to his feet. "Your mother," he said, gesturing broadly, "has recently educated me on the importance of making my true feelings known. I don't claim to have perfected the technique, but I am trying. I want you to know—all of you—that my criticism was always meant to be constructive, and I naturally had assumed that you understood...that it went without saying..." He shoved a hand through his hair and stumbled on. "For pity's sake, Roland, you have been my good right arm since you were scarcely more than a boy! You have performed every task, every responsibility, I have ever given you without so much as a stumble, and there have been many, many opportunities for failure. But never once have you disappointed me. What father could not love such a son as you?"

For a moment, Roland could only stare as tears thickened his throat and sheened his eyes. How long had he waited to hear those words? The truth was, he had never expected to. He couldn't think what to say, how to reply, but a kind of joy he had never hoped to experience bubbled up inside of him, and suddenly words were tumbling from his mouth, words that seemed to make light of the whole thing.

"Who are you and what have you done with my father?"

Roland winced at his own flippancy as Victor glared. Then, suddenly, Victor's face relaxed and he actually chortled, loosening chuckles from the others. "I suppose I deserved that," he said. "But your father is here, Roland, and offering you his love." He opened his arms, and Roland walked into them unhesitatingly.

"Father. Oh, Father." He wrapped his arms around the older man and hugged him tight. His father's embrace was equally strong and warm. Roland closed his eyes, savoring the moment as some part of him, some final little piece he hadn't even realized was missing, clicked into place.

"About Lily," he said at length, breaking away and blinking his eyes dry.

His mother had risen and come to stand with her arm about his father's waist.

"Do you love her?" she asked evenly.

"Yes."

"And does she love you?" Victor asked.

"I think so."

"I'd say definitely so," Elizabeth piped up. "I happen to know Lillian Montague, and if she came to your room as you say—and I don't doubt that she did—then she *must* be in love with you."

"Well, then," Victor said, linking his arm with Sara's, "as your mother and I want nothing more than for both of our sons to be as happily wed as we are, you have my wholehearted approval and blessing."

"And mine," Sara said, leaning forward to kiss Roland on the cheek. "She must be something, this Lily of yours."

"Oh, she is," Roland said, his heart swelling with a veritable bounty of joy only slightly dimmed by the manner in which he had parted from Lily. "Unfortunately, I have some misunderstandings to straighten out before I can consider myself formally engaged."

"I wouldn't worry too much about that," Rafe said. "You managed to convince Damon not to kill you, and that *after* he'd found you with his sister and you accused his family of kidnapping."

"Yes, indeed, a masterful piece of work, that. I begin to think we've underestimated your skill at diplomacy," Victor said. Looking past Roland to Rafe, he suggested, "Perhaps we should consider Roland for that newly created ambassadorship with the European Union."

"Oh, no!" Roland exclaimed, backing away and throwing up his hands. "I have plans of my own, thank you very much."

"And what, may a mother ask, would those be?" Sara queried.

"Lily and I are going to build a horse ranch."

"A horse ranch?" Victor echoed dubiously.

"Not just any horse ranch," Roland insisted, "the finest ranch with the finest horses in the world."

"But I need you here," Victor exclaimed.

"You have Rafe now."

"*He* needs you!" Victor insisted. "Who's going to be his good right hand if you leave us? I can't live forever, you know, and I've reached an age when I'm beginning to think about slowing down, spending some time with your mother and our grandchildren."

"You don't have any grandchildren, yet," Roland pointed out.

"Well, not quite," Rafe put in, coming to stand beside Roland. "But he's right, Father. We have a few years yet, surely. Perhaps, when we really need Roland, he'll be ready to come back to us."

Victor grimaced, and for a moment Roland expected him to dig in his heels, but then Sara squeezed his arm, and he closed his eyes, relenting. "Oh, all right, if you're sure that's what you want."

"Quite sure," Roland told him.

"But you won't rule out coming back into government at some later date?" Victor pressed.

Roland opened his mouth, intending to put nails in that particular coffin, and found to his surprise that he wasn't quite ready to do that. He'd have to discuss it with Lily, of course—given the chance—but until then, at least, he saw no reason to make blanket statements. "I'll, um, give it some thought."

"Good enough," Victor said with a decisive nod.

"Now then." Rafe clamped an arm around Roland's shoulders and cut him a grin. "What can we do to smooth your way with the Montagues?"

Roland shook his head. "I don't know. Unless I miss my guess, Charles is the real problem, and I can't imagine what it will take to appease him."

"Oh, I think we can handle Charles Montague," Victor said, showing his strong white teeth in a predatory smile. "Diplomacy is fine in its place, but a strong hand played at the right time is often more successful. Think about it, boys. Do we not have a bit of leverage?" With that, he looked meaningfully at his daughter-in-law.

Grasping something of his father's plan, Roland looked at his brother. "I'm not averse to threatening Charles," he said carefully, "but I wouldn't want to put Rafe and Elizabeth in a difficult position."

"Oh, it won't come to that," Victor assured him. "We'll just give old Charles a simple choice. All or nothing."

Rafe, who had been frowning in concentration, suddenly beamed. A full understanding of Victor's proposal hit Roland at precisely the same moment. "Father!" he gasped, completely overcome.

Victor Thorton's smile grew positively wolfish. "The old dog may have learned some new tricks," he said, "but he hasn't forgotten the ones he already knew, either. We'll have you and your Lily married right and tight the moment we know my daughter is safe."

Roland laughed and threw his arms around the two men

flanking him. "In that case," he said, "I have another favor to ask."

After he had put it to them, Victor and Rafe merely looked at each other, and then Rafe shrugged and said, "Consider it a wedding gift."

Dreams did come true. Now all Roland needed was a way to make Lily listen.

Damon stood in the doorway of her private sitting room and watched her for a long time, obviously choosing his words carefully. Disinterestedly, Lily turned back to contemplating the courtyard below from the window seat where she sat curled into a tight ball.

"Want to talk about it?" he finally asked.

She shook her head. "No point," she said morosely. "I already know how foolish I've been."

"Foolish in what way?" Damon asked, coming inside and closing the door.

She lifted one shoulder in a shrug. "How many are there?"

"You aren't reproaching yourself for not knowing who he was, are you?" Damon asked, languidly crossing the floor. "Because, I assure you, that bit of foolishness should more easily fit my head. I've been out and about a great deal more than you have, my girl, and I've seen Roland Thorton, all the Thortons, come to that. I knew he looked familiar, but I, um, had other things on my mind at the time, frankly."

Lily sighed. "It doesn't matter, Damon."

"It does if you're beating yourself up over this," he insisted, folding himself into a chair near the window, facing her. "Come on, Lil. How can I help you if you don't talk to me?"

"There's nothing to say."

"There is if you're as unhappy as you seem."

She frowned. "I'm not unhappy. I'm...disappointed."

"In Roland."

"And myself."

He leaned forward, elbows balanced on his knees. "Explain please, starting with Roland."

She fixed her gaze out the window. "Isn't it obvious? He lied to me."

"Um, we'll leave that for the moment because I'm quite sure you don't need me to point out that you lied to him as well."

"Meaning my lie cancels out his?" she demanded, hurt to have Roland's perfidy dismissed so easily—by her own brother, no less.

"I didn't say that. I merely said we should put that aside for the moment. Now tell me, what besides his concealment of his identity has occasioned this acute disappointment in him?"

"He's a Thorton!" she retorted.

Damon nodded. "Terrible, that. You know, though, I got a pretty good look at the fellow the other night, and I didn't see either horns or a tail."

Lily's mouth fell open. "It's not funny, Damon! You know the Thortons are mortal enemies."

Damon had the nerve to chuckle. "*Mortal enemies?* You really must get out more, sister mine. I don't think I've ever heard that particular phrase outside of the stage before."

"You know what he came here for!" she accused. "You know how he used me!"

"And I know why," Damon said calmly. "Honestly, Lil, can you expect him to just stand by and wring his hands while his sister has gone missing? I dare say, if it were you in the clutches of a kidnapper, I would move heaven and earth, play any role, grasp at any lead, to find you.''

Lily felt her face crumple. ''I know you're r-right,'' she managed to say, ''but why me? Do I have the word *fool* stamped on my forehead or something?''

''Nothing of the kind,'' he said, getting up and coming to sit on the window seat beside her. He wrapped his arms around her and pulled her close. ''You're not a fool, Lily. You've a pure heart and a clean soul, and you just naturally expect everyone else to be the same. I wish it could be so, for all our sakes, but, alas, it all too clearly is not. Otherwise, the world would never have heard of such knaves as Spencer and the ghoul who has Roland's sister.''

''But that's just it, Damon,'' Lily wept. ''I know all about the Spencers of the world, and yet I did it again. *I* went to *his* room—uninvited this time, so I can't even blame him. He told me almost from the beginning that he didn't believe in true love, that marriage seemed a cold and thankless business to him, but I was determined to prove otherwise. I fully meant…if you hadn't stopped me…''

''I may have stopped you from making love with the man,'' Damon said forthrightly, ''but I think you had already accomplished your goal before that night, Lily. I arrived in the courtyard in time to hear him declare himself quite firmly, you know.''

''*After* you caught us,'' she sniffed.

''Well, if you think I had anything to do with that exhibition he made there in the courtyard, you'd best think again, my dear. I confess that he put my most urgent concerns to rest almost at once. After your, um, rather dramatic departure, I frankly saw no reason for threats or what have you. What he did after that, he did wholly on his own.''

''Honestly?'' Lily asked, dabbing at her eyes with a seemingly ever-present handkerchief.

Damon lifted a hand, palm flat. "As God is my witness."

Lily pulled a deep, shuddering breath. She'd cried more in the past two days than in the whole of the past five years, and she did feel a little better now, but the situation still looked decidedly bleak.

"But what about Father?" she said. "He'd never forgive me if I married a Thorton."

Damon sighed. "That is a problem, I admit, but I, for one, refuse to view the Thortons as our enemies any longer. Father may not like it, but I intend to help them find their missing heir, if I can. Perhaps you and I together can change Father's perspective. If not and the opportunity arises, you'll just have to decide how important Roland Thorton is to you, Lily, and then live with the decision as best you may."

Lily felt fresh tears gathering. "That isn't as s-simple as it s-sounds," she blubbered. "We could both wind up disowned. How can I do that to someone I love? Ultimately, he'd have to resent that I cost him his family."

"So you do love him," Damon stated gently.

"I thought I did," Lily cried, "but I know I shouldn't! Oh, Damon, what am I going to do?"

Damon patted her back awkwardly. "I don't know, Lily," he told her honestly. "I wish I did. Unfortunately, I don't think anyone can answer that question but you. Whatever happens, though, I want you to know that you'll always have me. Always."

Lily wiped her nose with the limp linen handkerchief and kissed her brother's cheek before tucking her head beneath his chin and laying her head upon his shoulder. "Thank you, Damon."

"Least I could do, little one," he said, "the very least. You're my favorite sister, after all."

"I'm your *only* sister," she pointed out, chuckling reluctantly.

"Why, so you are," he quipped. "Funny how many of you there seem to be about the house at times."

She poked him in the ribs with her elbow. "I hope you aren't mistaking our slow-moving house guests with me."

"Hardly. It's shocking, isn't it?"

"What is?"

"How blatantly and often we've neglected them."

"And how they just keep staying on despite it," she pointed out drolly.

Damon's understanding had gone a long way toward raising her spirits, but as always Lily's thoughts turned to Roland. He had promised he would return for her, true. But would he? After all she had said and done, she couldn't really blame him if he never showed himself in this place again. And she wasn't at all certain that she had the strength to put aside her own fears and doubts in order to go with him if he came for her. She closed her eyes and wished with all her might that someone else could make these decisions for her. For the first time, she almost wished that she was sixteen again. It was so much easier to live with dreams than reality.

Chapter Ten

"And what is it that you think you're doing, boyo?"

Roland turned at the sound of the familiar voice and grinned cockily at the grizzled ostler. "I'm stabling my horse, old man. What does it look like?" Ignoring Jock's narrowed eyes, Roland turned back to latch the gate and hook his elbows over the top of the rail. "I'm calling him The Jolly Roger. He's a beauty, isn't he?" The massive black stud raised his sleek head and blew, as if being the center of attention was entirely his due. A single bracelet of white encircled the ankle of one strong foreleg, the only mark on the powerful beast.

Jock ambled up and hung his chin over the gate. "Aye, he's a fine looker, all right, but will he stay the course? Now there's the question."

Roland knew perfectly well that Jock was more concerned with the animal's owner than the horse itself. Taking no offense, he told the old man in no uncertain terms just what it was he wanted to know. "I love her, Jock. I'm not leaving here without her."

Jock paused a moment, then nodded with satisfaction and turned his gaze back to the horse. "It won't be easy, lad. She's terrible mixed up, our Lily."

"I think that's understandable."

"I think you should know why she lied to you and why I allowed it."

"You don't have to explain," Roland said. "She was protecting herself. That's obvious."

Jock nodded. "And now she's afraid her father will disown her if she goes with you."

"I can take care of Charles Montague," Roland told him, "and if I can just get Lily alone long enough to talk to her, I'm pretty sure I can straighten out everything between us, too, but I'm going to need a little help from you, my friend."

"And what makes you think I'll help you?" Jock asked, squinting his eyes into tiny slits.

"You love her, too," Roland said simply, "and you know I'll make her happy."

Jock looked away, but then he said, "You'd best take care of her father first."

"My thoughts exactly. He is here, isn't he?"

"Aye, he arrived last night."

"Excellent. Now all you have to do is get me in to see him."

Jock sighed and nodded and finally said, "You'd best tell me what you're planning then."

Roland clapped an arm across the old man's shoulders. "I'll do that, but first I want to ask you a personal question. You can think about it and give me your answer later. How would you like to head the finest stables in all the world?"

"Are you saying I don't?" Jock demanded, puffing up, and Roland had to laugh.

"All I'm saying is that Lillian and I are going to need

help making our dreams come true, and I can't think of anyone better for the job than you."

"Eh, well, when you put it like that," Jock said, rubbing his chin, "a man can't do less than think about it, can he?"

Roland grinned. "Aye," he said, adopting a thick brogue, "a man couldn't do less."

They almost ran into Damon in the hall. Roland would have stood his ground and met the challenge head-on, but Jock had already shoved him around a corner, hissing like a snake.

"Whi-hi-hi-hist! Are you daft, lad? Now is not the time for deciding which cock is lord of the yard. One rooster at a time."

Rolling his eyes, Roland folded his arms, clutching in one hand the cowboy hat he had used to obscure his features when trailing Jock past the guards. He waited until Jock peeked around the corner, signaled all was clear and motioned for him to follow. They stepped out onto the dark red carpet of the ornately gilded hallway. Roland found the castle rather overdone for his taste, especially the royal offices, but decor was not on his list of priorities. He strode down the hallway right on Jock's heels, almost bumping into the old man when he drew up in front of a pair of narrow doors.

"You wait in here," Jock whispered, "until I get rid of the footman stationed outside the prince's office door."

Roland nodded and slipped inside the room, taking in the small, uncluttered desk and delicate lyre-back chairs. A woman's office, possibly Lily's mother's. Jock scratched at the door, opened it and poked his head inside.

"What are you waiting on?" he groused irritably.

Roland glared, then followed the man out. Ten seconds later, they stood before another pair of doors, these tall and wide. Jock knocked, then opened one of the doors and stuck his head inside. ''And there you are,'' he said to the man inside, ''your important self returned from your world travels and nary a word to your old friend.''

''Jock! Come in. Come in.''

Jock thrust the door open and stepped through, signaling Roland with a surreptitious flip of one hand. ''Aye, and I've brought someone to see you,'' he said to the round man behind the enormous black-lacquer desk filigreed in gold leaf. ''And don't bother bellowing. I've sent the footman off.''

Charles Montague of Roxbury, a rotund, oddly unimpressive man with white hair rimming his bald pate and small glasses perched upon his nose, shoved back his chair and got to his feet. ''What the devil is this all about?''

''Charles, Prince of Roxbury, I give you Prince Roland of Thortonburg,'' Jock said by way of formal introduction.

''Thortonburg!'' Charles erupted.

''Aye, and I'd hear him out if I were you,'' Jock said calmly. ''He's got something you want, I vow, and likewise.'' With that, he turned and clapped Roland on the shoulder, whispering, ''That feisty darlin' o' yours will be outfitted and waiting—and Lily, too, or my name ain't Jock Browning.'' Snapping an insolent bow even as Charles blustered about proprieties and traitors and such, Jock backed out the door and closed it behind him.

''How dare you,'' Charles was saying, ''whoever you are! Prince Roland of Thortonburg, indeed. The Thortons are a ragtag bunch at best, but you're no more than a scruffy cowboy, certainly no prince of the realm, by God!''

Crossing the room, Roland tossed his cowboy hat onto an ebony bust resting atop a marble column, dropped into a chair and lifted his booted feet to prop them insolently on the corner of the desk. ''Now that's no way to speak to your future son-in-law,'' he said, and plucking from his shirt pocket a sheaf of folded papers backed in pale blue and secured with a ribbon, he tossed those onto the desk, as well, adding, ''especially when he's brought you deed and title to Thorton Shipping all tied up in a bundle with a nice, white bow.''

Charles Montague shut his mouth with an audible snap. For several long moments he stared at the papers on his desk. Then, as if afraid they'd bite him, he carefully pulled them toward him, tugged the ribbon loose and flipped them open. After scanning perhaps two paragraphs, he sat down again, dropping into his chair with a plop. Roland templed his fingers, smiled, and began to tell Prince Charles of Roxbury just exactly why he was going to allow a ''ragtag'' Thorton to marry his only daughter.

''He is magnificent, Jock,'' Lily said, studying the huge black stud in question. ''What did you say his name is?''

''The Jolly Roger.''

''Hmm, very piratical. I'd say it fits nicely. What I don't understand is how you came by him. Did Father bring him in last night? I can't believe he wouldn't have mentioned it.''

''Ah, no,'' Jock murmured, rubbing his chin. ''Fact is he came in this morning.''

''From where?''

''Ireland, I should think,'' Jock replied, squinting an eye at the animal huffing against the empty Western saddle and bags on his back. ''Mind you, he could be out of London or even Kentucky. I wasn't given provenance. But to my eye, he has the look of good Irish stock about him.''

''Right the first time,'' said a familiar voice.

Lily whirled to find Rollie—or rather, Roland—standing nonchalantly against the stall behind them, one elbow braced against the corner post, one ankle crossed negligently over the other, the toe of one boot driven against the cobblestone floor. He held a western hat of pale straw in one hand and wore a tentative smile, the hard look of purpose in his blue eyes. Lily's heart turned over.

"You!"

"I said I'd be back, and here I am."

She whirled away, excitement warring with doubt in her chest. "You brought this horse here," she demanded, "and then had Jock summon me to the stables?"

"I did." He crossed the aisle and shoved past her to open the gate and slip into the stall.

"Why, Jock?" she demanded of the old ostler as Roland gathered the reins from the cleat where they were tied, fit his boot into the stirrup and swung up into the saddle.

"Och, lass, it's for your own good," he said kindly, "just go with the lad."

"And why should I?"

"Because," Roland said, leaning a forearm atop the saddle horn, "I want to show you something important."

"And what would that be?" she asked with feigned disinterest, her heart hammering as he nudged the horse out of the stall.

"The future," he said, suddenly swooping down to clamp an arm about her and haul her up into the saddle with him. She yelped; the big horse blew and danced sideways in a show of spirit.

"Jock," she gasped, as Roland set her atop his thighs, "get me down from here!"

"Oh, I can't do that, lass," Jock said with patently false regret. "That big old brute there fair scares me to death."

"Which one?" she gritted out, clawing at Roland's arm. Jock merely laughed, and Roland nudged the horse into a reckless canter.

"I'll expect an answer when I get back, Jock," he called over his shoulder, "an affirmative answer."

"Aye, and I'm betting you'll get one," Jock said heartily, "perhaps more than one."

"Duck," Roland ordered just as they entered the tunnel of the archway.

Angrily marveling at the height at which they rode, she did just that, bending her head low as Rollie crouched over her protectively. An instant later they burst into the courtyard. She spied her brother just stepping through the side door that led to the car park and yelled at him.

"Damon!"

He looked up just as Roland heeled the big black and they lurched forward. As if shot out of a cannon, they were flying across the cobbles, leaping hedges and tearing up enough sod to make the gardeners go on strike. Before she could even catch her breath, they were streaking across the meadow.

She couldn't believe this was happening—or that they were out of sight of the castle before she even thought of truly fighting him.

"Stop! Let go of me! Let me down!"

"Not stopping," he grunted as her elbow connected with his ribs. "Be still before you fall!"

She knew he was right, but all the anguish, pain and confusion of the past days had overridden her good sense. "This is not Thortonburg!" she cried, struggling against the steel band of his arm. "I am a princess of Roxbury! I'll have you jailed! I'll have you *shot!*"

Roland abruptly hauled back on the reins and brought the big stud to a sliding halt. Unthinkingly, Lily threw her arms around Roland's neck in a bid for safety. Suddenly, she found herself nose to nose with him, her breasts flattened against his chest. Before she could gather her scattered wits, he kissed her.

The shock of his mouth against hers momentarily held her frozen, long enough for the old pull to reassert itself. Her eyelids fluttered as the whirlpool of desire sucked at her, beckoning her to surrender. But then the horse shifted and snorted impatiently, and pride rose on wings of indignation. She shoved at him, twisting her mouth from his. "My father will—"

"Your father has given me his blessing," he stated with maddening calm.

She snorted inelegantly at that. "He would never."

"I saw him this morning."

She stared at him, shoving hair off her shoulders. "I don't believe you."

"Think about it, Lily. Why would I lie to you?"

"I don't know. Why did you lie to me before?"

"Because I had no choice. What was your excuse?"

Stung, she put her nose in the air. He sighed and kneed the horse into a fast, steady gallop.

"Where are you taking me?" she demanded, her struggles mere tokens of her pique now.

"A place called Schooner's Point."

She gasped. "That's two hours from the castle."

"By road, perhaps. Jolly Roger will have us there in under an hour."

She renewed her struggles. "You can't do this!"

"Can't I?"

"Damon saw us. He'll be right on our heels."

"Jock will delay him."

"He wouldn't dare!"

"That man would dare anything to ensure your happiness."

"Well, this isn't the way to do it!" she exclaimed, perilously close to tears.

"It's the only way I could think of," he replied, and she knew he was right. Given a choice, she wouldn't have stayed in the same room with him this long. It was simply too painful. Straining a look over his shoulder, she saw not another soul. "Why don't you just relax and enjoy the ride?" he suggested silkily. "When we get there, you can throw a proper fit, if you want."

Lily narrowed her eyes at him. A proper fit, indeed. She'd show him a proper fit. Lapsing into sullen silence, she determined to conserve her strength for the battle ahead. Roland attempted to get her speak to him from time to time, but then gave up, proclaiming that conversation could wait until they reached the point, and so they rode on in silence, minute after long minute, while she fought the growing urge to relax against him and let the warmth of his arms soothe her jangled nerves.

The horse was mythic, Pegasus without wings, his stamina seemingly unending, his gait sure and steady and level. Lily grudgingly marveled. What a sire he would make, a lynchpin upon which a great equine dynasty could be founded. Roland would do very well with this one, provided he really meant to establish his breeding ranch. She couldn't believe that he didn't. The kind of enthusiasm he had exhibited when describing his dream simply couldn't be feigned. At least, she didn't want to believe that it could be. Understandably, she was having a little difficulty discerning between pretense and reality at the moment.

She was riding safe in the arms of a man with whom she had believed herself in love, except she hadn't known who he was, and he hadn't known who she was, and how could anyone be in love with someone she didn't know? But if she wasn't in love with him, why had she grieved his absence so? Why did she want nothing more than to lay her head against his shoulder and weep with relief? Why was she praying, inanely, that her father had, indeed, given him his blessing when she knew that such a thing was a virtual impossibility? Suddenly she wanted to lash out at him for the simple reason that he had made her hope. It was precisely then that the point came into view.

Roland kicked the horse into a faster gait. Amazingly, the big stud neither faltered nor hesitated, just stretched out and picked up his pace. Roland slowed him again as they drew nearer the grassy point that fell away on two sides to sheer escarpment and jutted out over a shallow cove where the waves rolled in to wash a narrow, sandy beach in timeless rhythm. Ten minutes later, they dismounted, Lily sliding to the ground first. She expected to feel a sense of freedom and mollification; instead, she felt oddly alone. While Rollie tended to the horse—loosening the saddle girth, then digging a shallow hole in the ground with the heel of his boot, lining it with a square of vinyl from his saddle bag and filling it with water—Lily stood staring out to sea, hugging herself lest she fly apart, bit by bit broken away by a myriad of conflicting emotions. When at last he joined her, he had a pair of binoculars in hand.

Standing at her side, he lifted the binoculars to his face and swept the seascape until he found what he wanted. Carefully, he adjusted the focus. "Ah, there it is." He lowered the binoculars and pointed out to sea toward Thortonburg, which Lily knew lay just beyond the horizon. "Here, have a look. Right there."

He offered her the binoculars, but Lily was in no mood for sightseeing. She turned her head away, shifting her weight from one foot to another, and ignored him. To her dismay and irritation, he stepped behind her, encircled her with his arms and gently nudged her head around, lifting the binoculars to her face.

"It's right over in there," he said, as she rolled her eyes, lashes brushing the glass. "Come on, Lily. We've ridden all this way. Just take a look."

Sighing, telling herself that she'd do anything to put some distance between them again, she wrenched the binoculars from his grasp, stepped forward and looked in the direction he had pointed. A moment later she found it, a small island, green with vegetation and rimmed with narrow, tan beaches just below the horizon.

"Do you see it?"

"I see an island, if that's what you mean." She thrust the binoculars at him and stepped a little farther away.

"Not just any island," he said, taking the binoculars from her, "*our* island."

She cut him a look. "You're insane, you know that, don't you? *We* don't have an island. *We* don't have anything. In fact, there is no *we.* And you would be wise to be long gone by the time my brother finds me."

Roland shook his head and carried the binoculars back to where the horse was now grazing placidly, punching them down into the bag tied behind the saddle. "*That,*" he said sternly, "is the island where we are going to live and raise our horses. It's a Thortonburg principality, but—"

Lily put her head back and laughed. "Why can't you get it through that thick skull of yours that *we* are a figment of your imagination."

"And why can't you get it through your pretty head that I love you?" he countered, walking back toward her.

She looked at Roland, Prince of Thortonburg, and suddenly all the grief and anger and disappointment and fear and doubt burst out of her, and she flew at him, fists flailing, a cry of pure anguish tearing out of her. He caught her against him, braced his feet wide apart and simply held on until the fury played itself out, subsiding into sobs.

For a long while, he merely held her close, crooning senselessly. Then, gradually, he began to kiss her, first her forehead, then her eyes and nose and cheeks, and finally her mouth. Passion blazed where fury had railed only moments before, and she could no more stop herself from lifting her arms about his neck and pressing herself against him than she could have stopped the tears or the anger or the hope that flickered to life within her.

He locked one arm across the small of her back, splayed a hand to cradle her head, and kissed her with tongue and teeth and lips and heart. It was as if he meant to lay to rest with this single kiss not only her resistance but all her doubts and fears, as well. And he very nearly succeeded. Nearly, but not quite. By the time he released her, she was beyond denying to either of them that she loved him still.

"Why are you doing this?" she wept. "We have too much against us."

"No, my darling," he said, sliding his arms loosely about her shoulders. "We have nothing against us, nothing and no one. That's what I was trying to tell you earlier. I spoke to your father. He really has given his blessing."

She had to close her mouth to ask the obvious questions. "But how? Why? It doesn't make any sense!"

"You can ask him that yourself—after you agree to marry me." He fished something from his jeans pocket and held it up to the light. A diamond of immense size and brilliance caught the sun and trapped it. "This belonged to my grandmother. My parents gave it to me when they gave me the deed to the island."

Lily reached for the ring, stopping herself only at the last moment. Her head was spinning, but one or two pertinent questions surfaced. "Did they know you were going to give it to me?"

"Yes."

"And they agreed?"

"They did more than merely agree, sweetheart. They wished us well and bade me welcome you to the family until they can do so themselves."

Lily could only gape wonderingly as he took her hand in his and slipped the ring onto her finger. It was a little large, but she closed her fist around it. "B-but you s-said you'd never...that you didn't believe—"

"And you showed me what a fool I was," he said, lifting her fisted hand and kissing it. "You said once that you could teach me to believe in love, but you already had. Lily, that night you came to me, I already knew. With your family's involvement in my sister's kidnapping ruled out, I had no more reason to stay—except you. I'd determined to tell you the truth of my identity the very next time I saw you and beg you to marry me, but then you showed up in that delectable dress and started your hot little striptease and all I could think of was making love to you."

"Roland," she whispered. "Is it true? You really love me, and my father and your family..."

"All true, sweetheart," he promised. "All that's left is for you to say that you love me and that you'll marry me. Then, as soon as my sister's safe, you and Jock and I can get about building that horse ranch."

She threw her arms around him, squeezing his neck so tightly that he was soon gasping for breath. "Oh, Rollie, Roland, whoever you are, I do love you!"

Laughing, he locked his arms around her and hoisted her off her feet. It was then that Lily caught sight of three figures galloping across the grassland toward them, one quite close.

"They've caught up with us," she said breathlessly, and lifted an arm high over her head to wave.

Roland whirled around with her still in his arms just as Damon fought his horse to a halt. Grinning, Roland dropped her to her feet, keeping an arm about her waist. Damon literally vaulted from the saddle and in two strides had clamped a hand around Lily's wrist and yanked her free of Roland's hold.

"Are you all right?" he asked her, glaring at Roland.

"Of course, she's all right," Roland answered for her. "She's more than all right. She's just agreed to marry me. I think."

"We'll see about that." Damon pulled her around to face him, saying, "Lily, you don't have to do this. We'll give back the shipping company. Father had no right to barter you like—"

Lily pulled away from him and brought her hands to her hips. "What are you talking about? What shipping company?"

"Thorton Shipping," Roland answered again. "I gave it to your father to end the feud."

Charles and Jock galloped up then and came to a skidding halt. Charles sat huffing in the saddle as if he had carried the horse instead of the other way around. Any other time, Lily would have taken the opportunity to upbraid him about his weight and lack of exercise. As it was, she had other things on her mind. "Is it true, Father? Did Roland give you Thorton shipping?"

"Yes," Charles huffed.

"On the condition that he give his approval to your marriage," Damon added. "*And* he threatened him with permanent exclusion from the Wynborough contract."

Lily whirled to face Roland. "Is this true?"

"Yes."

"But how is that possible?"

He shrugged negligently, staring daggers at Damon. "My sister-in-law, Princess Elizabeth, got her father to agree to award the contract exclusively to Thorton Shipping."

"And you gave Thorton Shipping to my father," she clarified.

"Yes. To end the feud."

"So my father would give his permission for our marriage."

"Yes."

"But," Charles interjected, puffing still, "as usual your brother fought me on it."

"I won't have her bartered like stocks on the open market!" Damon roared.

"No one's bartering anything," Roland retorted hotly. "I gave your father Thorton Shipping in order to end the feud and win his permission for the marriage. Whether she accepts me or not is entirely up to Lily."

"That's right," Charles said, finally getting his breath and pulling himself up to his somewhat less than regal height. "The choice is Lillian's and Lillian's alone. So what's it to be, child? Do you want this Thorton? Do you love him?"

Lily had been watching Roland from the corner of her eye, admiring the way he stood his ground against her very intimidating older brother, while her heart melted with the knowledge of all he'd done to make it right for them. He had convinced the Thortons to give up their shipping company, to deed him their own private island, to welcome her into their family, even to offer her his grandmother's ring. She lifted her hand and looked down at the magnificent diamond on her finger, and she wanted to laugh, to fling her arms wide and embrace the whole, wonderful world, but that joy was too precious, too hard won, to share at the moment. So she simply said, "I want him. I love him."

She offered her hand, the diamond sparkling, to Roland. He caught it and with one sharp tug pulled her against him, his arms closing about her, whispering, "Lily. Oh, my Lily."

She laughed then, the joy too much to contain, and he kissed her, long and deeply, until Jock climbed down off his horse, cleared his throat and clamped a hand on Roland's shoulder, saying, "I think it's time you showed me this island of yours, boyo. If I'm going to build you the world's finest stable, I'd best see all there is to see, hadn't I?"

"What's this?" Charles demanded, easing his bulk to the ground. "What island? And what stable?"

"Come along, and we might tell you, your irritable highness," Jock said.

Laughing, Roland pulled away to fetch the binoculars and point out the tiny speck below the horizon. When he caught Lily's hand, intending to pull her along with them, Damon caught the other. "Ah, I'd like a private word with my sister."

Roland narrowed a warning glare at Damon, but then he dropped a kiss on Lily's lips, squeezed her hand and let it go. She beamed at him as he walked away with Jock and her father, the pair of them squabbling like the children they were at heart.

As soon as she turned her attention to Damon, he seized her by both shoulders, locked eyes with her and asked softly, "You're sure?"

Smiling wistfully, she nodded. "I'm sure."

"No more doubts?"

She shook her head. "None."

Finally, he offered her a tentative smile. "If you're really happy, then I'm happy for you."

She slid her arms around him and hugged him. "Thank you."

"Oh, dear," he said, hugging her tight, "my baby sister's about to become a married woman."

"Poor Damon," she teased, pulling back slightly, "now Mother will have only you to train her guns upon."

Damon groaned. "You had to remind me."

Lily laughed. "Maybe we can keep her busy for a time with wedding plans."

"Dare I hope for a huge production?"

"Dare we hope for anything else?" Lily retorted wryly. "You know Mother."

"Well, I'm a firm believer in giving mothers their due," Roland said, appearing at her side to lift a loving hand to the nape of her neck and gently pull her away from Damon and into his own arms, "but this wedding will have one time constraint and one only."

"And that is?" Damon asked.

"Finding my sister," Roland replied, sobering.

"You'll keep me informed and let me know if I can help?" Damon said.

"If you like."

Damon nodded. "Yes. It, um, seems appropriate now that we're going to be family."

"Family," Lily said, splitting a look between the two of them as they shook hands. Arguably, they were the two handsomest men who had ever lived, but she had never dreamed that one day they, a Montague and a Thorton, would be family by marriage, and she never dreamed that she would be at the core of it. Love had made a fool of her once before. Now love would make her a wife, bring an old feud to an end, and grow dreams into reality.

She spared a thought then, in the midst of her joy, for the sister-in-law she had yet to meet. She looked at the clasped hands of the two men who, between them, filled her heart to overflowing, and she knew, deep down, that the kidnapped Thorton daughter had at least two true champions on her side.

Family. Yes. It was right, and it was good. What evil, what fears, what doubts could stand against men such as these, against love such as this? Not hers, certainly. Roland's sister, she decided, was as good as home—and so was she. Smiling, she laid her head on her future husband's shoulder.

So was she. Home.

* * * * *

Turn the page
for a sneak preview of

A ROYAL MARRIAGE

by rising star
Cara Colter,

on sale in Silhouette Romance
in April 2000.

As ROYALLY WED *continues,*
a skeleton in the Thortons' closet
rears its head!

"My sister is missing," Rachel Rockford told the young constable. She could hear the strain in her own voice.

"Sir?" the man said, looking past Rachel, his tone brimming with both defiance and eagerness to be of service. Out of the corner of her eye she saw that a well-dressed man was now beside her at the counter.

"Good evening," the man said. His voice was deep and pleasing, the confidence he exuded evident in his tone. "My name is Damon Montague."

"*Prince* Damon Montague?" the man asked.

"I couldn't help but overhear the young lady's sister is missing. She seems to be feeling some distress. I think that warrants your attention far more than an antenna broken off my vehicle."

"I think there's something wrong," Rachel said, beseeching the constable with her eyes. "My sister Victoria usually tells me when she's going away. Her neighbor said she had gone away, but that she should have been back by now. I'm telling you, my sister is missing. Please,'' she said, ''please help me.''

And help came. From the most unexpected of sources. Suddenly she felt the brush of Damon Montague's expensive overcoat against her shoulder, and saw a glove quickly slipped from the strong and warm hand that covered hers.

The sensation was shocking, unexpectedly delightful. How long since anyone had offered her such a simple human gesture of support? How long since she had been touched?

Far too long. All the stresses and strains of single motherhood now seemed to be pushing from behind her eyes, too, this tenderness from a stranger breaking the dam of control she had built around her heart.

She felt the first tear slip down her cheek, and yanked her hand out from under the weight of his to brush it away. She fished in her pocket for a tissue. Her fingers felt a baby soother, and a crushed bonnet. Desperately, she considered blowing her nose in that, when a handkerchief was pressed into her hand.

She looked up at this man beside her. The gentle kindness in his eyes made her want to weep anew.

''Thank you,'' she said, and dabbed at her running nose and eyes.

''Miss, we need you to answer some questions.''

The pure monotony of being asked such routine questions as her correct street address and Victoria's helped Rachel regain her composure.

''I'm fine now,'' she said quietly to the man beside her once the questioning was done. She stared at the now used handkerchief, uncertain what to do with it. She certainly didn't want to return it to him in this condition.

''Keep it,'' he said, reading her mind.

''Thank you.'' Two thank-yous in two minutes. If he did

not go soon, she'd end up owing her life to him. That was the game she and Victoria used to play. If one did the other a kind turn three times in a row, then the other would say, jokingly, "Now I owe you my life."

Prince Montague did not leave, and she was glad for that.

"Perhaps it wouldn't be too much trouble for you to stop by—did you say Victoria?—Victoria's place of residence and ask a few questions.

"Well?" Montague prodded the constable, his voice so low that Rachel glanced up at him. There was no kindness in those eyes now. They were cold and hard. He was a man obviously very used to authority, to diffidence, to obedience.

"We'll do whatever we can, sir."

"Thank you," Montague said. He turned to her, and his eyes were warm again, sympathetic.

"Please. Allow me to see you home."

"No, I couldn't possibly. My car—"

"I'll have one of my staff return the car to you."

"Really, no."

"Rachel, I'll take you where you need to go. I just want to play knight to your damsel in distress. What do you say?"

No wonder this encounter was catching her so offguard. She was vulnerable. She surrendered. "I'd like a ride home very much, Your Highness."

"My friends call me Damon."

"I don't think we qualify as friends."

"Maybe not yet. But we will."

He found her utterly lovely, the woman who sat beside him in the car. Her hair was tucked behind her ears, and there were little white drops attached to tiny earlobes.

Earlobes that begged a man's lips to nuzzle them.

The thought shocked him. Since his wife's death, just over a year ago, he'd been walking in a fog, held in the grip of a grief so deep he was convinced it would never heal. Of course, it wasn't just the loss of his wife.

Sharon had died bearing their first child, a son. The infant, perfectly formed, a tiny, angelic replica of Sharon, had died, too.

He knew that people thought he had everything. And once that might have been true. But the fact was, tragedy had made him long to be the most ordinary of men. Because money, position, prestige—none of it could buy him out of this place he was in. A place of feelings so raw and overwhelming, he did not know what to do with them. And now his position was making demands on him to get better. Get over it. Get on with life. Do his duty.

"Is something wrong?" Rachel asked softly.

"No," he lied, and then realized he had wasted an opportunity. His offer to drive her home was motivated not just by a sense of wanting to help her, but a desire to know more about her missing sister.

What kind of coincidence was it that Rachel's sister, a young woman from Thortonburg, had gone missing in the very same time frame as the illegitimate daughter of the Grand Duke of Thortonburg?

Damon had pledged to help find the kidnapped woman, if it was within his power.

He shook his head slightly, smiled wryly at himself.

An old monk, Brother Raymond, whom Damon had begun to visit regularly since his wife and son's deaths kept telling him to look for the miracle. Kept claiming that eventually good would come out of Damon's tragedy. Told him, so emphatically, with such enviable faith, that nothing, *nothing,* in God's world ever happened by accident.

Damon had not believed it.

And yet tonight, sitting with this quiet woman he did not know, he felt it for the first time. Not quite a premonition. More like a glimmer. Yes, a glimmer of his becoming a man bigger and deeper than the man he was before. And even more oddly, a glimmer that the future held promise. And hope. And that somehow that was connected to this beautiful and shy stranger who sat with such quiet composure beside him as his car pierced the night.